TRIPLE
DOUBLE

JAMES LEWIS

Fulton Books, Inc.
Meadville, PA

Published by Fulton Books 2020

The artwork on the front and back covers are original works by southern California artist Jesse Fabian Mendivil. Jesse began drawing as a toddler and has been involved with art since. He started oil painting about fifteen years ago and his passions are portraiture and figurative art. You can find more of his work at jessemendivilarts.com. For inquiries please contact paintingwithjesse@gmail.com.

ISBN 978-1-64654-226-0 (paperback)
ISBN 978-1-64654-227-7 (digital)

Printed in the United States of America

This writing is dedicated to my parent's, Jack and Lynn and my Wife of many years Donna.

Acknowledgments

The Author would like to thank, many times over, the following friends that contributed their knowledge to this Mystery.

Terry Rice, a miner's, miner.

Ariel Mendivil, computer guru and Word pro.

I used the combined knowledge of three different Deputies, Scott Landen, Julie Landen and Randy Wortman. They rescued my, lack of law enforcement rules, so many times, it's close to a personal embarrassment.

The Bravo award goes to two friends. Frank Guarino and Bob Howard. They knew of my laziness and kept the writing flowing through their many persistent encouragements.

Piercing bright lights. Barely audible mechanical sounds. An odor akin to cleaning fluids. His eyes began to register the light and a strange new environment. First reactions began with a wariness of his surroundings then an inherent alert to be on guard. His eyes hadn't fully opened, nor had his hearing been tested, for several days and nights. In a coma, his mind was beginning to move forward. But he was still lost in a cloud of confusion for several long seconds. As his eyes began to focus, new questions were coming to fruition. He thought, *Am I alone? Are those hospital noises?* Abron tried to speak out loud, at least he thought he had. There were more questions. *Why can't I wake up? Where am I?* Up to this point in his short life, he had never imagined himself asking that oldest of stunned phrases.

He tried moving his hand to feel skin, but someone or something was holding him down. *Both arms and legs seem to have feeling,* he thought. *Why can't I move? Why can't I see?* Again, that gnawing thought, *Where am I?*

"Mr. Kelsey, I can hear you," said a strange voice. Abron Kelsey—tall, strong, athletic—was a man with a hard face, deep-blue eyes, and brown hair. He was currently lying immobilized and numb in body and mind, trying to listen while searching within the maze of his slowly awakening thought process for answers. He was reclined, immobile, dazed, and in physical and mental pain.

He began to realize that no amount of education or past experience could help him. Abron thought out loud, "Patience. I think that was a voice." It was unfamiliar. Real or not, his head was splitting with pain—pain so intense he involuntarily yelled then screamed. And then the lights went out.

*****

The call came in from a neighbor just south of what would become a crime scene. It was a report of shots fired at a home nestled up to the shore of Newman Lake, Washington. Deputies Terry Hollander and Mike Gwen were the first investigators on the property. Local law enforcement had cordoned off the driveway moments before they arrived. The neighbors that had reported hearing shots were standing with the police on the graveled dirt road. Newman Lake was surrounded by heavy forestation. Only a couple of roads were paved.

After Gwen and Hollander questioned the neighbors, both went under the tape and approached the breezeway separating house and garage. Detective Gwen was the first to spot the body lying in the kitchen. Both deputies drew their weapons and entered through the unlocked windowed door. Crouching, they slowly cleared the home and met at the body. "Call CSI, ask for Christian and that new guy Kelsey to come ASAP. She's dead, but I don't see a gunshot wound."

After the call, Terry and Mike slipped back out the door into the breezeway. Slowly opening the garage-side door, they were both awestruck with what was hanging in plain sight. A second body, that of a male, was suspended from the rafters by his hands. Blood was everywhere. He had been shot, stabbed, and cut many times. A brand-new white Mercedes was parked to one side of the garage. Sergeant Gwen commented, "No blood splatters on the car. Unusual." The deputies returned to the road and the police, explaining just enough to warrant a blockage of the property from prying eyes. The sheriff's department took over and waited for their CSI unit. The deputies again questioned the neighbors, gaining identity of who the house belonged too. Both knew the deceased, if the bodies were those of the homeowners.

Gwen commented to Terry, "I don't think our department has ever seen anything like this—two prominent lawyers beaten and butchered in their own house."

Terry added, "Maybe we should sit on it until Saunders gives a go-ahead?" They both agreed. Now the CSI unit would try to piece the puzzle together.

*****

The Bump Inn at Coeur d'Alene, Idaho, was Abron's and his fellow deputies' haunt. An occasional beer in hand, case conversations, and stratagems were the norm. Over the state line from Washington, ideas could take many different paths. Work interventions seemed far away. The Bump, a pub and grill, was loud and fun. The posse was, for the most part, invisible. They were quiet and nonoffensive, and no uniforms allowed. Their lack of hairstyle or, for that matter, lack of hair altogether was the only giveaway.

They all shared in the conversations. Here, lines could be crossed, laws slightly bent, in their talk of ongoing investigations. Information sharing was paramount to these get-togethers. The deputies looked forward to them. Nothing was held back, even criticisms aimed at each other. Over the first few months of these exchanges, Abron Kelsey could point out the barfly regulars, sizing them up by occupation and attitude. Even during conversations at his own table, he would catch the slightest personal clues through the actions of people at the bar or seated throughout the club. He and his fellow officers stayed out of trouble, even swallowing the occasional insult from young inebriated college students. Abron Kelsey, twenty-six years old and single, was looking for a relationship. His eye for detail was not wasted on a petite short-haired blond bartender. She only worked Monday through Thursday, which was puzzling. The crowds and the tips were always more plentiful on weekends.

Abron had only been working for the Spokane Sheriff's Department for a couple of months. One cold winter night in late November, with snow on the ground, the officers were discussing a particularly brutal crime scene inside a home on the shore of Newman Lake, east of Spokane. Two attorneys had been killed mercilessly. One had been hung, shot, and stabbed; the other, clubbed and stabbed. David McCoy was found suspended from the rafters in the garage. His wife's, Assistant District Attorney Phyllis McCoy's, body was discovered on the kitchen floor, inside the house. The investigation was just beginning. The Bump was quieter that night, due to the cold outdoor conditions.

Abron stood up and said, "Coffee time, the road home will be slick."

As he turned toward the bar, Christian Caine from the forensics lab whispered, "Here he goes again." All eyes surveilled his approach to the bar.

"Ms., may I order six coffees to go?" The young lady bartender couldn't help noticing Abron's confident yet courteous vocal demeanor.

"Four minutes to brew, one more to deliver," she replied, not looking up or turning in his direction.

"Thank you," he said.

The young lady bartender was Isabel. This was just one of her part-time jobs and interests. Isabel Davis was enrolled at Eastern Washington State College, out of Cheney, south of Spokane. Attending classes during the morning and early afternoon hours, she had little time to dawdle. What Abron and the others didn't know was that Ms. Davis also tended the bar at the Davenport Hotel in Downtown Spokane on weekends. With her energy and interest in people, Isabel made both bars fun stops for guests with her quick wit, outgoing personality, and baby-doll looks. Her apartment and college were closer to the weekend work. Isabel was majoring in sociology, with a minor in Northwest history. Surprisingly (and to her, at times) annoyingly, she possessed a gift not unlike Abron's. Isabel Davis continually evaluated people around her by way of their actions and reactions. Isabel Davis was averaging about twelve units per semester. After four years of study and bartending, graduation was finally in sight. She was starting to feel anxious about her new vocation and the challenges that lay before her.

Quickly standing up to help the lady he wanted to meet, Abron said, "Let me help you with those."

"Whoa partner," she snapped, "this is a balancing act that took me a while to command." Isabel made a show out of setting the coffee on the table. Her quick verbal response to Kelsey was not expected but liked. "I didn't mean to be so abrupt," she said and followed with "We could have made a pretty large mess if they tipped."

We, Abron thought, perving. Abron paid and tipped her then asked, "Why not weekends?"

Again, a quick retort. "Study time." Knowing exactly where he was coming from, Isabel said, "I'm still a helpless starving student at Eastern Washington."

As she turned to leave, Abron chanced an introduction, shouting over Carlos Santana's "Smooth," "My name is Abron. May I know yours?"

Isabel made another show out of turning slowly to face him. With a smile and big hazel eyes staring into his, she replied, "Yes, I'm Isabel. My friends call me Izzy."

A little in the moment, there was a pause; Abron was caught in her stare and beauty by surprise. Quickly he thought, *I can't miss this chance.* Abron's voice erupted over the music. "May I call you Izzy?"

Without pause she shot back, "No."

Terry, Ron, Mike, nor Christian would not look at Abron. They were all forcefully trying to hide chuckles and grins. Mr. Big had been shot down by a five-foot, one-inch fireball of a bartender. For Abron, it would be weeks before he would talk to her again.

*****

Another change was taking place in the inner circle of the Spokane sheriff deputies seated at Bump that night. Mike Gwen's transfer to the San Bernardino County Sheriff's Office had come through. He would be leaving in less than two weeks. Gwen was much liked by his fellow deputies. They admired his sense of doggedness on all cases he was assigned. His teammates also knew he could bench-press over four hundred pounds and run a mile in under five minutes. Abron Kelsey had become a close friend in the short time they had worked together. The two officers coordinated their weekly visits to the gym. Abron would miss Mike's entire family. Kelsey was not used to the togetherness and love shown by all four toward each other. The loss of this deputy would be tough to get used to. The Gwen family had practically adopted him when he came to town. The team had one last round of coffee then headed home for the Thanksgiving weekend with their families. Each deputy had two days off and two on for the holiday.

As they departed the Inn, the posse stepped into a brutally cold howling wind that let them know winter had come to town. When struck by the twenty-degree temperature and a wind-chill factor, all immediate cares disappeared. Only one thought presented itself: hurrying to the safety of their cars. Kelsey was hesitant to leave the parking lot and head back west to his condo. Would it be right for me to go back and talk with Isabel? Or would it be wrong to force the issue. He put the car in reverse. *I am not a stalker,* he thought. Inside the Bump, Isabel was wondering if she would ever get to know the mannerly cop.

*****

On the other side of the parking lot, hidden among the few cars that were weathering the cold, another member of the posse was closing their car door and starting the car. Detective Terry Hollander was casing the parking lot, waiting for the heater to work. He was suspicious of everyone. Terry had come out of the Army after four years of OJT with the military police. Terry had met his future wife in Germany while stationed there. Gretta was magnificent. Athletic, blond, and gorgeous, she loved Terry for his manners, chiseled face, and stability. Struggling through unhappy teen years, she was a product of a broken home. Her dad was away on business for weeks at a time. Her mother had turned alcoholic, bringing many boyfriends home in his absences. Gretta learned, at a young age, to stay in her room or over at a friend's house while Dad was away. Terry Hollander was just what she was looking for in her eighteenth year. He was her rock. When the letter arrived from America, Gretta's pulse had quickened. It had been almost a month since he mustered out of the military. The plane ticket fell out first: a plane ticket to Spokane, Washington. The Spokane that her lover and best friend had described so many times. Just a few words were written on the note: "Please marry me. I love you. Terry."

Only Gretta's dad and two closest girlfriends attended the wedding in America. But the church was full. Dozens upon dozens of Hollander's family and friends were present. Gretta was a hit—graceful, beautiful, and commanding a broken English pattern of speech that enchanted her to everyone. She was blessed with caring friends and a father that loved her. Gretta and Mike Gwen's wife, Debbie, were inseparable. For Gretta, the goodbyes would be exceptionally hard. When she first met Debbie and Mike, she was alone while Terry worked. Debbie Gwen had introduced her to many people and a busy schedule of local clubs and organizations that filled her days. Pondering the Gwens' departure, Gretta thought, "I'm losing one of my best friends. With the internet and Skype, I'll still be able to show Tammy my bump." A few short weeks after Debbie and Mike departed for California, Terry was given the news by Gretta. Their "passion in the woods" on the way home from the Gwens' anniversary party nine weeks earlier would soon add a new member to their budding family.

*****

It was at the Bump Inn that Sergeant Terry Hollander began the story of Rose Lake to Kelsey. Gwen was two weeks gone. "Abron, you weren't on the force two years ago when the first double homicide occurred in our area." Kelsey stared at Terry with a keen interest. "The victims were the Nelsons—a father and son that resided on a farm between Rose and Killarney Lakes in Idaho. The case was not in our jurisdiction but the CDA Sheriff's Department asked for us to cooperate. Like Newman Lake, the Nelsons were, for lack of a better term, butchered. The father, Joe, was found hanging by his hands from the rafters—shot and cut many times all over his body. His throat was slit when the bastards were through with him. The son was found in the meadow behind the house, shot in the back. His throat had also been slit. To this day there have been no arrests. Until now it had become, not cold but warm for the CDA Sheriff's. I think you can understand why our team has a lot more on its plate than just Newman Lake. Obviously, these double homicides could be related."

The information was just sinking in when Christian's phone rang. "Thank you," he said then turned toward Kelsey. "Abron, I thought you might want to visit the crime scene at Rose Lake, so I requested permission from Lieutenant Bara over at CDA. That was him. We're on for tomorrow morning at ten. There are some notes I wanted to go over at the lab before we meet. I'll catch up with you at the crime scene." Christian handed Abron a map with the address and location circled and notated.

Abron Kelsey had earned a degree in forensic sciences from the University of Washington before entering the police academy and joining the Spokane sheriff team. Prior to college, he had served a three-year enlistment in the Marine corps. The former USMC sergeant had proven his worth in the corps through a tour of duty during the war on terrorism in the Middle East. Now, employed as a deputy assigned to forensics, he was making use of his remaining education benefits by attending night classes. Someday, these classes could lead him down a new path—possibly a law degree from Gonzaga. Physically, Abron was an imposing presence in any room. Mentally, he was constantly honing his skills through education. What most male acquaintances missed at first, the ladies did not. They feasted on his sentiment, sensitivity, and muscles. His parents nested in Charleston, just south of Coos Bay, Oregon. Soon-to-be retired, they were looking forward to visiting the eastern side of Washington State and their only child.

*****

Abron's mind was working overtime during his drive back to the apartment. *Copycat? So many similarities. Had to be the same persons involved.* Knowing his job was forensic evidence, Abron couldn't help but wonder about the cases in their entirety. Arriving home, his thoughts wandered pleasantly to the sassy little blond that he wanted to call Izzy. Maybe someday she would allow him to use her nickname. She was beautiful to him in many ways—looks, charm, wit, and "in-charge" attitude. In Abron's personal life files, Isabel was his number 1 priority. His next move would be to wrangle her phone number and find out more about her availability, likes, and dislikes. How could something so easy be so complicated for him? *I'll see her soon,* he thought, looking forward to their next encounter. His thoughts slipped back to Christian and Rose Lake. The job was growing more interesting day by day. Before turning out the night-light, Kelsey summed up his many experiences over his short lifetime. *Patience* was the word he was searching for. His ability to wait and observe would serve him well.

Abron was up early. From his apartment complex, it was a short walk to the little café.

"Good morning," Joan said as Abron took in his favorite aromas. Joan talked to Abron almost daily. "Corn beef and hash, sourdough toast, coffee, and lots of honey?" Joan had been serving Abron breakfast since he moved into the neighborhood. She knew he was a cop of some type, but Kelsey never wore a uniform. He was a good tipper, and his conversation was educated. He led with "Did you watch *Magnum* last night?" already knowing the answer.

"I love that man. Not the original but still a hunk" was Joan's smiling reply. She poured him some coffee. Officer Kelsey was stalling by reading the paper, doing the crossword, and checking out how the Spokane Flyers had skated the night before. He didn't want to be too far ahead of Christian. The overnight snowfall had left several inches on the street. He could already visualize I-90. The snowplows would have it cleared by now, all the way to the St. Maries cutoff. Paying his bill and usual tip, Abron began to make his move toward the door.

Joan asked, "Busy day?"

The deputy replied, "First stop CDA."

She then, for the first time, acknowledged his job. "Be safe, keep your head down. See you on Monday." She smiled.

*****

Christian arrived at the farm about ten fifteen—a few minutes late but in time to have possibly saved Abron's life. The scene was bloody. Christian made the call: "Officer down." There was no chance of seeing the license plate on the Ford pickup now slamming away from the barn. "Need ambulance and backup. Abron Kelsey has been beaten and shot. Waste no time getting it here." Christian chanced another quick glance out the side door and saw the outlines of two riders in the pickup, both with baseball-style hats. The perps were hunched over, offering little chance to be identified. Caine knew his Glock would be ineffective at that distance. The amount of blood already soaking his friend's clothes sent him into a frantic search for the open wounds. There was no time to waste. It was life-and-death.

Christian immediately turned the wounded deputy on to his side, momentarily taking away the chance of Abron choking on his own blood. Worrying about a broken neck or spine in those first few minutes, Christian held the officer's head as still as possible. Every action taken was to save Abron's life. Talking to the downed deputy was of no use. Christian pressed his gloves into the stomach wound; there wasn't even a groan. While trying to cover the wounded man, Christian's adrenaline rush had subsided. Fortunately, inside the walls, the air was still. Covering Abron with his own winter coat, Christian began to shiver. It took almost thirty minutes for an ambulance and more deputies to arrive. Caine could now testify to just how cold it was in that lightly lit freezer of a barn.

*****

Shoshone County deputies from Wallace and Kellogg were first on the scene after the "Officer down" call. The local deputies were ten minutes ahead of the Coeur d'Alene responders who had to navigate the icy Fourth of July pass. Holding on to the stomach compression, Christian gave as much information to the first responders as he could, including a good description of the white getaway Ford pickup. Less than a minute later, the next patrol car arrived. The first patrol car took chase down the dirt road headed south toward St. Maries. While in pursuit, an APB was sent out to all Idaho, Montana, and Washington jurisdictions. Both officers giving chase knew it would be like looking for a needle in a haystack. Lost time and eroding winter road conditions would make it close to impossible. Sleet falling turned to heavy snow and blizzard-like conditions. As the officers headed south on the paved highway, they realized it was too late for tracks. Snowfall had taken its toll, blanketing the highway in the last fifteen minutes.

As Abron was being taken from the scene unconscious, Christian had no idea whether Kelsey would live long enough to make it to the hospital by ambulance. The snow and low ceiling wouldn't allow helicopter transport. Detectives Ron Rowe and Terry Hollander pulled in and went straight to the barn area where the shooting occurred. The detectives found the north-facing side door ajar with just a skiff of snow on the ground, in the area shaded by the north-facing overhang. Two sets of footprints were entrenched. Four feet away from the outside wall, the tracks quickly disappeared. The POIs wore the same type of boot, leaving deep tread marks embedded in the mud, snow, and ice. The escape route was easy to follow. Disappearing prints led to where the pickup had been parked before the attack. "Do you think Abron heard that pickup arrive?" asked Ron.

It was Christian who answered. "No way. He was hit on the back of the neck and head while crouched down, then they shot him. Another few seconds, and they would have finished him on the spot. I think my arrival made them bolt."

"From a stone-cold crime scene to red-hot. We now have persons of interest," stated Terry. "And they're both wearing the same brand of boots. Call the chief. Let him know all three of us are here and on it. Maybe he can buy us more time in Idaho to find out the reasoning for the attack." Ron made the call.

*****

Christian was taller than Abron by an inch. Constantly in a struggle to stay below 240 pounds, he had just spent 8 weeks dieting down to 227 with noticeably more energy at the lower weight. Maybe, he thought, shedding more weight down to 215 would enhance his physical abilities to an even greater extent. The elevator battle he was constantly waging stemmed from one source: a must in his life, Tammy. Tammy was Italian, and Tammy could cook. With an inheritance, the first item she bought for their house was a two-tiered brick-lined oven that stood five feet tall. Every kid in the neighborhood knew when she was baking Italian bread. The kids would knock on the side door in pretense of asking Tammy and Christian's twins if they could come out and play. When she opened the door, Tammy always had a platter of fresh bread, buttered and straight out of the oven. The twins, Cody and Jody, were younger than most of their half-dozen neighborhood playmates. The siblings were thrilled every time they heard the knock on the side door. It was playtime! In years to come, the twins would become as important as the bread. Theirs was a tight bond.

Christian's take-home pay allowed Tammy to be a stay-at-home mom. She didn't take the nicety for granted. Her thoughts were on the other mothers in the neighborhood, PTA meetings, baby showers, birthdays, luncheons, etc. Mrs. Caine knew most of the other moms worked full- or part-time jobs. Christian didn't care one way or the other. He liked to eat—chicken cacciatore, veal piccata, lasagna, Italian meatballs. Tammy knew Christian loved linguini over spaghetti, so it was always linguini. For his birthdays, she strayed from Italian cuisine and would make his "favorite dish of all time," as he would say—beef stroganoff with extra sour cream. The local butcher always sold her prime-grade filet mignon to use in her dish. *After all,* he thought, *she's cooking for Lieutenant Christian Caine.* If Christian worked out every day of his life and took half portions each time he ate, he just might stay under three hundred pounds.

*****

Terry and Christian were the first to arrive at the hospital on day 7 of Abron's hospitalization. His head was immobilized with a cage, pins anchoring it to his skull. He could, however, finally move his arms and legs slightly. Kelsey had asked a nurse for a mirror to see how extensive the cage was surrounding his head. All he could do was try to whistle when he saw the metal anchor screws. Terry spoke first. "How does it feel to be incarcerated?" Terry and Christian were grinning.

Abron tried to smile, murmuring "How long?"

"This is your seventh day, my friend," replied Terry.

"A lot has taken place since your ambush. New connections have opened-up, too, for all four killings our department is involved with," said Christian.

A third voice spoke. "No more questions. Dr. Marsh just instructed me to limit everyone's time spent with Abron. Right now, I need some time alone with Deputy Kelsey," bellowed their captain. Terry and Christian were outgunned. They quickly said their goodbyes, vowing to return later that evening.

"Christian already filled me in on why you two visited the Rose Lake crime scene. When he notified me of your meeting, I cleared it with Captain Croop and Lieutenant Bara at CDASD. My question, before your attack, would have been, what was to be gained? Obviously, the result was brilliant police work that almost got you killed. The two of you tipped somebody's hand. At the same time, you gave our department greater autonomy at Rose Lake. You guys seem to have stirred up the proverbial hornet's nest."

"Captain," whispered Abron, "traces of opiate and hidden room."

"Are you sure about the presents of opiates?" asked Saunders. Kelsey blinked assent. "I'm calling in Terry and Ron to debrief you tomorrow morning. Should Christian be present?"

"Yes" came Abron's slur.

"Rest while you can. Take your meds, and pay close attention to Scott, your rehab guy. He's the best in the business. You're probably a couple of weeks out from Scott. Listen to him when you start. He can work wonders with his knowledge and methods. As I said, the boys will be in to start a report on your crime scene and attackers.

The next morning, Terry, Ron, and Christian entered Abron's room. He was just finishing up his liquid diet and cut fruit. "Good morning, are you ready for us?" Ron questioned. Kelsey blinked assent. The officers kept it short, realizing again just how badly Abron had been injured. "They came in via a dirt road that runs along the river. The tire tracks had the same studded tires on the rear drivers as the prints over at Neuman Lake." Terry was trying to give Abron some positive information. Abron's head was beginning the early stages of a massive migraine. Kelsey began to convulse. The officers wasted no time bringing assistance. Less than thirty seconds later, Kelsey was lost to the world thanks to the cocktail the nurse shot him full of.

"I hope he can get over these episodes," commented Ron. The deputies were shaking their heads as they departed his room.

*****

Sergeant Mike Gwen was a little taken aback at the size of the county abutting Los Angeles. His new territory ran all the way east to the Colorado River at Needles and down the river south to Parker Dam. Detectives Rowe and Hollander had sent information on the double homicides, coupling it with a report on Deputy Kelsey's attack and injuries, to all agencies in the Great Northwest and to Gwen personally. They received a dozen hits for more information from Salt Lake to Portland, Seattle, and even from Shelby, Montana. This morning it was Sergeant Gwen's email that stood out. Gwen mainly wanted to know if his friend was going to survive. Kelsey's and Gwen's personalities had bonded immediately when they first met. Mike had been trying to get up to speed with the San Bernardino County Sheriff's Department when the news arrived about Abron's brush with death. The news would have to wait until the end of the day. Important training overruled his questions for the immediate now.

Sergeant Gwen had not dealt with the harshness of gang activity as found in his new county of work.

Today he was being schooled along with several other deputies. Every day he was gaining in knowledge and confidence. There were drugs, drive-by shootings, prostitution, even a terrorist attack by a man and women claiming to be aligned with ISIS. The two had senselessly murdered over a dozen American patriots busy doing their everyday jobs. Mike appreciated the highly organized sheriff's department. They were adept and armed with information and special training programs to help combat city, county and inland empire crime. Every day Mike looked forward to briefings and assignments. It was a busy world of law enforcement at his new position.

Late that afternoon, sitting in front of the computer, the reply took less than two minutes after his inquiry. "Officer Gwen, Abron out of danger, full recover expected. When can we have a beer?" It was emailed by Terry Hollander.

*****

Ron Rowe had been partnered with Terry Hollander for some time. Through their many investigations, they had worked out ways to tackle different situations as they occurred. Detective Rowe joined the Spokane Sheriff's Office right out of high school and the police academy. Ron was one of Captain Saunders's first recruits. Saunders admired Ron's attitude toward his duties. Before he captured the full scope of Ron's abilities, Shawn had already aligned him as a kindred spirit. Both officers had a love of the Northwest, fishing, hunting, camping, skiing, motorcycles, snowmobiles, and speed boats. Two kids in the same office. One thirty years the senior.

Ron came from a loving family with both parents solidly entrenched in life around Kamiah, Idaho. With six siblings, his communications skills were inbred. Ron would someday have a large family. Unfortunately, Ms. Right, hadn't come along yet. His dad first brought Ron's attention to his ways. "You're a deputy, son. Why all the drinking and carousing? Your mom and I think you need to join a church. Maybe then you'll find a loving wife." Ron believed his dad and took his advice. He didn't stop at one church. Ron began attending three regularly. Young Officer Rowe figured that his chances of finding a wife were much greater that way. *But she has to know how to fly fish, wet and dry.* He would marry someday. Right now, the outdoors and chasing several ladies at once were too much fun. Just before winter had set in, Rowe helped a gal move into the apartment next to his. Recently divorced, she had two small kids. Over the next few weeks, all four would become close.

*****

Isabel had been skiing at Schweitzer Basin over in Idaho when the accident occurred. She was about to sit down on the chairlift when a boy standing next to her slipped, causing Isabel's ski to turn. Down she went, twisting her foot 180 degrees as the chair banged into her and her riding partner. It was a serious accident. Within five hours Isabel Davis was on the operating table having two of her ankle bones fastened back together with plates and metal screws.

Just out of recovery, Izzy was rolled into her own hospital room that looked more like a New Year Eve's celebration. Her parents and a dozen of her friends were waiting for the patient. Isabel was reminded that today was her birthday. Fortunately for her, one week later, school could continue with the use of the internet and her parents. Isabel's retired mom and dad lived less than a half mile from her apartment. Unfortunately, she couldn't work for a while. The two bartending gigs were here first love, her sanity outlet. Izzy was a people person. Her recovery had afforded her more idle time than she was used to. Settling into a routine with her close friends, the crutches, Izzy started each morning with a cup of coffee and time on the internet. At the beginning of the third week of her rehab, she was perusing the local news when she read "Spokane officer seriously injured while investigating a crime scene near Rose Lake, Idaho." Reading further, "Deputy Abron Kelsey was beaten and shot. Listed in critical condition at a Spokane-area hospital. No further details available at this time, pending investigation."

Isabel's mom was hit with a call, in seconds. She didn't know what to think. Isabel had never been as interested in seeing someone, especially "right this minute"—"Please, Mom, let's leave for the hospital as soon as you and Dad can pick me up." With snow still on the roadway, Isabel's father drove all three to the hospital. Isabel asked at the desk labeled "Information" about Abron.

"No visitors allowed," she was told. "Officer Kelsey has an armed guard day and night."

Isabel then asked, "Is he out of surgery? Is he awake? Can he speak? Can he walk?"

The hospital employee in charge of the front desk explained, "Unless you're immediate family or law enforcement, no admittance, no details."

A man's voice, behind Izzy and her parents, asked, "Aren't you Izzy the bartender out at Bumps?" Isabel turned to see Ron Rowe smiling at her. "Hey, we've missed you, but it's obvious you can't bartend on those crutches."

Izzy interrupted. "Is he okay? Can I see Abron? Can you get me into his room?" she asked.

"Are you carrying any concealed weapons? You were pretty tough on him the last time we all saw you."

Izzy blushed. For the first time, her mom and dad understood. "Isabel," said Ron, "he's in pretty rough shape—swollen, discolored. He has metal screws in his head that hold a cage built to keep his neck from moving. I can get you in, but it's not pretty."

"I don't care about that. I want to see him and him see me."

*****

Isabel was given clearance into intensive care. Her parents waited in the visitor room. Isabel gasped when she saw how extensive the injuries appeared. Abron's eyes slowly came alive when he saw her. But there was no movement other than that. As she drew nearer, Dr. Marsh entered, nodded to Isabel, and asked his patient if he had regained any more feeling and/or movement in his arms and legs.

Softly, Abron answered, gutting out a "Yes."

"Can I speak to you in front of the young lady?" asked Dr. Marsh.

Izzy said, "I was just leaving."

Abron spoke, whispering "Stay." She sat down.

Dr. Marsh began. "The bullet missed your vital organs but nipped an artery, which we repaired. The artery opening was small enough that we were able to use a stent device to repair it. Your downtime should be no more than four weeks. But I caution you, its four weeks before you can leave the hospital. That doesn't include rehab and rest. Your neck and head are far more serious. We had to truss you up in that headgear to give your neck bone time to repair itself. Fortunately, the crack was small and should knit enough to lose the headgear in that same four-week period. This type of break could have been much more serious if your detective friend hadn't stabilized your head and neck when he found you.

"The MRI results on your skull show a crack. Our team had to drill holes on both sides of your brain cavity to drain fluids that were causing pressure buildup, giving you those monster headaches. You'll need several more MRIs and a CAT scan or two before we're through with you. We can't diagnose the full extent of your concussion. Only time will tell."

"Crippled?" Abron asked.

"No, in three or four months you'll be good as new physically. Mentally, we have to wait and see. By the way," the doctor said with a poorly disguised wink to Izzy, "some of the nurses are wondering who your personal trainer is. It seems you've attracted some volunteers among our nursing staff." Abron got it. So did Isabel sitting quietly nearby. "Get some rest, and keep your calorie count up. I'll check on you tomorrow."

"Thanks," Abron muttered.

Dr. Marsh left the room, and Isabel said, "I'm glad I got to see and officially meet you while you're bedridden. Will I need to ask all these nurses if I need an appointment next time?" She smiled.

Abron replied, "See me."

Isabel Davis then stated, "When I lose the crutches, it'll be you who can't catch up with me." Abron grinned as best he could. She added, "You now know where I work, both jobs. You also know where I attend school. If you can't find me, ask a detective." Before he could reply, Isabel asked, "May I visit you tomorrow?"

Izzy's parents were awestruck. This was the first time their daughter had shown any meaningful interest in a man. As the three departed the hospital, Isabel's mom asked, "May I drive you back here tomorrow? And can you introduce me to this mystery hunk?"

"Please, Mom, and yes, tomorrow." Izzy didn't know if it was maternal, her need to help the injured, or (and she thought for a minute) "love." Then she told Grace, "I can't get enough of him. Just being around that guy makes me happy. I know he looked distorted, lying there. But he is a very handsome man. I can't believe I could fall for an overgrown policeman that told me he was in forensics, and that's all I know of him." Never having had this experience before, she wondered what to do about it. "Mom, would you have Dad do one of his famous searches to find out more about Abron? I think he might be worth it, but I don't want any surprises! He mentioned the Marine corps and college, which would make him several years older than me. He's had plenty of time to be married, have kids, murder someone, or maybe my intuition is telling me the truth. He's witty, smart, handsome, sexy, and available."

On the drive home, Izzy asked, "Would you stop at that bookstore for a few minutes?" As her parents waited outside, she bought a book for Abron.

*****

One week later, Isabel introduced her parents to Abron. After small talk, and as if on a sign, both ladies visited the restroom just down the hall. Jack Davis stayed and asked Abron about his injuries and his background. He knew he hadn't much time and tried to balance his questions to not sound like an investigator. Jack used some sleight of hand in his questioning, asking Abron about Huskies football and his military duties before questioning him about his parents, his siblings, and past marriages. Abron tried not to show he was on to him, answering every question while infusing signs of still being groggy from all the meds. Kelsey was struggling with his head and neck brace when the ladies returned, and the questioning took a back seat. Isabel's clearance through the guard allowed her to enter and exit as needed, with or without guests.

Jack wished Abron a speedy recover. He and Grace departed to the waiting room. Abron's mind was much sharper than the week before. He smiled and asked, "Would it be too bold of me to ask if I can call you Izzy?"

"Since you obviously can't do me any harm in your condition and I enjoy talking to you, I think cop jargon would be 'That's an affirmative.'"

Finally, Abron thought, *first base.* Who would have thought it would take nearly two months to arrive here?

Isabel then asked, "How are you feeling today?"

With Abron, talking to young ladies was not his greatest attribute. "Much better, thank you. I was able to stand and walk on my own earlier. The doc assigned a rehab specialist for my recovery. I start this afternoon with all muscles below my shoulders."

Izzy chimed, "I thought most of a policeman's muscles were located above the shoulders next to the doughnut storage."

Now he laughed out loud and quipped, "Izzy, sheriff's department employees are deputies, not policemen." Changing the subject, he said, "How about yourself? Can you still bartend? Do you have to go into rehab? And are you free for dinner the day I get this contraption off my head and neck?" He caught her off guard.

"I don't know where to start, Abron. Good, yes, yes, and I'll look forward to dinner. I do bartend seven nights a week. My doctor had a walking cast fitted. Behind the bar, I'm now hell on wheels." Then she added, "Both jobs owe me some time off. Seriously, if you're asking me for a date, yes, I would love to."

Abron was smitten. To himself, he thought, *What a beautiful woman.*

Izzy quickly changed the subject and asked, "Can you remember anything about the day you were attacked?"

"Izzy, I think there were two of them because I'm sure I heard a gun go off as I was going into unconsciousness. I think the culprits were there searching for something. I noticed a lot of dirt had been shoveled, raked, and generally moved around where they clobbered me. But, Izzy, I'd rather talk about you."

"Ask away," she replied.

"How young are you?"

"Twenty-two and old enough to know better than to give my real age." She smirked. Then she asked, "How old are you?"

"Fair enough, I'll be twenty-seven in two months."

"Officer, I mean, Deputy, you're twenty-six and not giving me a straight answer. It wasn't a trick question," she said.

Abron said, "I'm a very young twenty-six in all ways except thinking. Education forces me to act older in keeping up with the career."

To which Izzy replied, "Well, act your age, and don't ever ask a woman hers." Isabel then queried him about a next-day visit. Kelsey smiled and nodded assent. Isabel departed to join her parents, who were waiting down the hallway.

Riding the elevator down to the main lobby, Isabel spouted an abrupt "Damn, I forgot to give him the book." She stayed on the elevator and headed back up without her parents. As the door opened, a loud bang went off. The officer guarding Kelsey's room fell off the chair, hitting the ground while grabbing his midsection. A moment later, as nurses, patients, and visitors were panicking and running away from the shot fired, an armed security guard, weapon drawn, started yelling orders as he ran toward the scene. "Get back, clear the area!" he yelled as he slammed through the confused workers and visitors.

"Freeze," he shouted. "Hands where I can see them." Isabel, in shock, raised her hands. Izzy was positioned on her knees next to the two bodies. The floor was turning a crimson red when the guard backed Isabel away. She was trying to talk, trying to explain, but her words weren't making much sense. The guard was the first to see the movement. He grabbed the gun lying next to the bodies. Slowly the patient, wearing a neck brace, began to push the shooter off him. With a sorrowful pain-induced voice, Abron spoke. "Don't hurt her. She's my friend." Isabel began to sob.

*****

Later that day, sheriff's deputies Rice and Monroe were filling there captain in on the shooting of both wounded lawmen and the deceased. "No identification on the perp. The officer is going to survive. He took a bullet to the midsection. Policeman Waltz was seriously lucky. The surgeon's report said the bullet missed his spine and caused no life-threatening injuries to his stomach and intestines. When we interviewed Abron, he acted like the event was all in a day's work. Kelsey also took a bullet that went through his hand, changing the path of the bullet away from him toward the wall. The hand has a hole in it but, miraculously, missed bone. Fortunately for Isabel and two nurses, they all had just departed his room before the shooting started.

"Apparently, Abron was stepping out of the bathroom when the first shot gave warning, sending him into attack mode. He was crouched behind the door, partially hidden. Kelsey said the gun hand came through the door first. That's when he grabbed it, as the weapon was discharging. What happened next is almost superhuman. Abron crushed the attacker's skull with a heavy metal-based IV stand. The follow-through sent both to the ground as Isabel Davis entered the room."

"Abron's jolt, when he hit the floor, opened the wounds on his head where the cage is attached. The blood from his hand wound added to the mess he made of the attacker. We stayed until Abron was patched up and the results of his MRI became available. Dr. Marsh said Abron was lucky. Again. No new damage to his vertebra. He should still have the same range of motion after the soreness abates. Time will tell with his total healing."

Captain Saunders replied, "I never saw this coming. Apparently, the Rose Lake killings are hiding something much larger than anyone thought. Isabel, is she okay?"

Deputy Monroe answered, "In shock. Her parents were downstairs and took her home. We thought it best to get her away from there. Pat and I set up a meeting with her tomorrow morning. We posted a deputy at the door and added a second Spokane police officer by the elevator door on his level. The deceased attacker will take time to identify. No ID found. His face is all but gone."

*****

In 1889, a halfway house with a bar, rooms to rent, an eatery, and a horse stable opened in Idaho territory. It was located a couple of miles from where the south and the north fork of the Coeur d'Alene River met. The way station was called the Saddle Inn. Over the years and a few generations later, it came to be known as the Silver Saddle. People would stop there while headed east or west along what is now Interstate 90. In the late nineteenth century, the territory was showing the first signs of development leading to statehood. It was a wild land that was growing in population thanks to the mining and logging industries in the region. The railroad came through around the turn of century, and commerce took off. Many of the early miners struck it big with the silver and gold unearthed from their claims. Fortunes also were made by selling earlier staked claims. Late arrivals made money opening stores and presenting services the workers and families needed. The first owner of the Saddle Inn was a hard foul-mouthed woman named Molly. She believed in shaking loose every penny possible from her customers.

Molly was blessed with a devilish smile and thin anatomy. Born in Ireland, Molly was one of the best-known early pioneers of the region.

In the late spring of her first year in business, a couple of tough-looking cowboys checked into a room, paying for three days in advance. The unsmiling cowboys were riding two Appaloosa ponies and leading six empty pack mules. They boarded with Molly's workers. All eight animals were in good condition, just needing hay and rest. These cowboys liked their steak rare, whiskey to drink, and loud bawdy talk. The two paid for everything with silver coins. Molly and her hired men couldn't come up with any answers concerning the empty pack mules. Molly understood the wagon trail from Montana into Idaho was in good condition. For so many pack mules, one cargo hauler would have been the better choice. It piqued her interest.

On the first night of the boys' stay, while they were drinking in the saloon portion of the inn, Molly introduced herself. Recognizing their slightly inebriated condition, she fell into a conversation, asking about their journey through Idaho territory all the while complimenting them on their youthful looks and manners. Their glasses were never empty. Molly was entrancing that evening. With long brown hair and in her late thirties, she always wore low-cut blouses. Later that night in their room, after both men had passed out, she quietly slipped on her skirt and flannel shirt then started in on their saddlebags. She smiled when she found a half-dozen gold coins and a few gold nuggets the size of small marbles. Molly also found a hand-drawn map with two marks of interest. The first mark was near Butte, Montana. The second x was between what later became known as the Rose and Killarney Lakes. That second mark was not more than a half-day buggy ride from her inn.

Molly took one nugget and one gold coin from the small pull-string pouch that contained the twenty-dollar gold pieces. It was way more money than these young toughs could have earned, legally, in two or three years. She replaced the map and slowly slipped out of their room. When she was downstairs, she drew the map from memory and put it in her safe. The young riders were gone most of the second day, returning after dark. Both were so exhausted they passed up Molly's advances. Henry, Molly's stable hand and confidant, reported that the horses and pack mules had been ridden hard. On the third day of their stay, just before dawn, both riders and their animals were gone.

News arrived slowly in the late 1800s until the telegraph and railways were constructed. The Saddle Inn became a hub of information. Molly foresaw the benefits of being a postmaster while also offering a telegraph service inside her establishment. A month after the two cowboys had departed, news came of a train robbery out of Butte, Montana. The robbery, shoot-out, and escape had taken place just two weeks before the two young riders had stayed at the Saddle. The stolen items were more than interesting to Molly: three hundred pounds of unrefined gold, six thousand dollars in gold coin, and stores of laudanum and opium medicines. Within three days, map in hand, Henry and Molly had a buggy packed and ready to travel. Henry was not just a stable boss. He could handle any rifle or pistol that was available. Preferring to settle most of the Saddle Inn's problems with brute strength and fisticuffs, Henry was big and tough.

Molly and Henry traveled southwest, following the river. As the north fork turned straight south toward St. Maries, a logging township, darkness fell. They slept on the ground and waited for dawn. At first light, Henry started a fire, boiling water for coffee and frying bacon. Molly perused the map once again. Together, they agreed on a meadow and canyon that lay halfway between the Rose and Killarney Lakes. Already on the east side of the river, they followed a wheel-worn path south again toward St. Maries. Soon they found a less-used wheel trail that ran back east off the main southern route. It showed signs of recent usage. Twenty minutes in, they entered a meadow. Henry was first to spot several men working about a quarter mile across the open area. He halted the buggy while they were still hidden in the trees. "That's why the path is so worn. Someone is building something."

"Do we want them to know we're here?" asked Molly.

"I'm sure they didn't see us," he told Molly. "I'll get on up that hill to where I have a view. Keep the horses as quiet as you can. I won't be long." The hill was more like a cliff for the first fifty feet. Henry used the outcropping of roots and rocks to scale the escarpment. When on top, he walked up the slope another hundred yards and slowly edged toward the meadow overlook.

It was too far to hear anything except the occasional loud noise of unloading some crates and metal objects from a wagon team just inside the tree line. Henry did spot a peculiar-looking cleared area on the south edge of the meadow. The clearing was worn and looked to have a used ashen firepit. Next to the pit was an odd-looking arrangement of rocks circling what looked to be a well. If it was a water well, somebody had dug it out. The dry summer would have been in the laborers favor. Henry knew the work put into that well had to have covered many weeks. The rim was a good six feet across. Who knows how deep it was? Two small canvas tarps were draped over poles to provide shade and shelter for the men in the meadow.

When he returned to where he'd left Molly and the buggy, Henry reported everything he had seen. He was sure only three men were working. "It might be the start of a sawmill, but it's hard to say," he said, adding, "I think we should spend the rest of the day getting to a vantage point on the south side. It overlooks what seems to be a campsite. We could use some time watching and listening to their chatter." Henry tied the horse team out of earshot from the wagon path. Fed and watered, they would be fine until morning. Both horses were tethered lightly in case a mountain lion showed up.

*****

"The Newman Lake murders have similarities to Rose Lake. Ron and I feel something else is afoot," Terry began.

"Theory?" asked Captain Saunders.

"Newman Lake was payback, motivated by one of the victims' occupation. We believe only one of the McCoys was targeted. Phyllis and David McCoy were posed for law enforcement benefit," Terry replied.

"Whoever killed the Nelsons would, in no way, want to bring more heat to a cold case. A case so cold that all of law enforcement had given up looking for the motives or the perps. All CDA sheriff's findings from Rose Lake point to torture of the deceased father, Joe, as a tool for gathering information. Joe Nelson was still alive for some time while suspended. The coroner's report points to torn muscles in his abdominal area, shoulders, and neck. He was probably trying to defend himself by flailing his body hanging above the ground."

"Christian questioned the doctor who did the autopsy on Phyllis and David. Phyllis was brain-dead before she hit the ground. The stab wounds were for effect. The autopsy on David showed no signs of struggle. He died before being hung by his hands in the garage. The cause of death is listed as a bullet to the heart. The McCoy killings may not have been a copycat."

"Have you reported any of this to Captain Croop or her team?"

"No, sir. We have certain suspicions and need more time before letting our thoughts become theirs. With your permission?"

Saunders nodded his approval. "Are you getting any new information from CDA's people?" asked the captain.

"Drug deal and manufacturing equals illicit cash. That heads their list. Same old stuff. Like somebody's suppressing information. Abron told us yesterday in the hospital that he thought the crime scene and investigation went south too quickly." Abron's attack and subsequent discovery of the underground room reopened the case to the CDA and the Spokane Sheriff's Department.

"Ron and I both agree the attack and murders were over something greater than we are seeing. Certainly more valuable than the small cache of drugs found on the premises. And why the brazen second attack at the hospital?"

"Chief, can our team get more freedom to investigate in Idaho?"

"I'll contact Terry Croop this morning" was his reply. "CDA's captain is not afraid of jurisdictional overlap. Make sure you question every neighbor in the area, even if they just moved in. I'm shifting Abron to your team. He can't be pushed physically for a while. Use his knowledge of the law and forensic abilities to your advantage. Try to find out who the Nelsons did business with, including grocery shopping, locals, and their routines. Let's hope our person-of-interest list grows substantially. Remember to keep CDA's man, Lieutenant Bara, in the loop. I'll handle all calls to Ms. Croop," cautioned Saunders. "FYI, their theory, when you rule out drugs, brings our own aluminum refinery in to play. Both Nelsons worked there. Do not get caught up with the idea that both double homicides aren't related. You, Ron, and Abron are now a team in this."

Terry Hollander had worked closely with Ron Rowe before. Kelsey was a newbie. Captain Saunders would use his new lieutenant, Jake Monroe, to lead the investigation of the McCoys. Detective Pat Price would be his partner. Saunders foresaw promotions within his department and new hiring to bring his force up to the tasks at hand. His search began for seasoned detectives available within the Pacific Northwest. "Gwen would have been perfect for the task," he uttered out loud.

Before departing the captain's office, Terry asked, "Any updates on Abron's condition?"

Shawn answered, "I've never dealt with anything like this, or for that matter, I've never even heard of an incident like this except in the movies. To be shot while recovering from injuries—he shouldn't have survived in the first place. Imagine how quickly his mind and body had to react to save himself from his attacker! Abron had an IV in his arm attached to the metal stand he used.

"Add to that a neck and head brace screwed into his skull. Fortunately, the new bullet hole to his hand is the least of his injuries. Kelsey summoned so much strength for that strike it opened his midsection wound and twisted the head brace beyond repair. He went through a refitting with no painkillers, just a local deadener. Amazingly, he's none worse for the wear. As far as being able to begin his duties, Dr. Marsh said he expects him to stay on the same schedule he had until fully recovered, just like the attack never happened. Officer Hollander, you can quote me on this—Abron Kelsey will be at his desk, working, in less than four weeks no matter how hard we try to keep him away from the station."

"When we ID his attacker, it should lead to who's behind our unsolved double homicides."

"I'm guessing the assassin is either Union or an acquaintance of the Nelsons and/or McCoys." Terry Hollander and Ron Rowe had a lot on their plates: Rose Lake, Newman Lake, and Abron's attackers. Both detectives wondered about the hiring of Lieutenant Jake Monroe. Making the new deputy the lead investigator of the Newman Lake incident left them scratching their heads. They both liked the personality, but he was an unknown when it came time for working in the trenches.

*****

Hollander had never met the Nelsons or McCoys. His and Ron's thoroughness in studying their backgrounds and case files would come in handy many times over the course of their investigation. The second attempt on Abron's life left a body and little else. The dead assassin was dark-skinned, probably of Mexican descent. No tats, no scars, clean-shaven. Hollander wondered if the attempt was caused by something as simple as a dispute with a neighbor. More likely, somebody paid the perp to finish up what they started at Rose Lake. The investigation would take months. Terry muttered to himself, "I'd best pay attention." Cynthia Berdot, Spokane's assistant DA, had phoned the station the morning she was told of a head-to-head with the CDA sheriff's office and Segeant Terry Hollander. "Ms. Berdot, this is Terry Hollander from the Spokane Sheriff's Office returning your call."

"Deputy Hollander, I'm in charge of the Nelson files that have to do with Washington." Cynthia was to the point and abrupt. In her forties, she had no time for small talk. "I need a report on your meeting with the CDA people on my desk tomorrow morning. Can you handle that?"

What an asshole, Terry thought to himself. "I'll have Captain Saunders fax it over after he reads it."

"I said, it needs to be on my desk first thing."

Hollander quickly decided his course of action. "Take it up with the captain. Anything else?" The phone clicked off in his ear. *That was interesting,* he thought to himself. *Nelsons instead of the McCoy homicides?* Seeking an opinion, Sergeant Hollander phoned the hospital. Abron Kelsey was the department's underground railway to legal information.

"Shouldn't she be talking to Shawn or Croop or the Idaho DA's office?" Abron's answer was sketchy, at best. "To my knowledge, there are no laws covering her asking for details. I think it's odd to put you on the spot like that without the consent of either captain. I hope this helps, but I've read nothing to the contrary."

"Thanks, Abron, get well." Terry ended the call.

Kelsey's mind was unstoppable. Now, new fodder had been presented with this information. Along with everything else the case consisted of, a theory was beginning to take shape. His patience and diligence were just what the captain needed from him at this stage of the game.

*****

Communicating in a Bump Inn atmosphere was far different from the confines of the Spokane office. Since Terry had been promoted to lieutenant, another new name was assigned to their team, Detective Pat Price. The trio had been invited into the evidence room at CDASD. Idaho's crime scene investigators were making it available to them after the Kelsey incident. Lieutenant Bara would meet them, offering an overview of his detectives' findings. North Idaho's CSI team was blessed with several cerebral civilians, or eggheads as law enforcement liked to call them. The evidence room offered up at least a dozen boxes involved with the Nelson killings. A new shelf in the room was dedicated to Officer Kelsey's attack. Ron, Terry, and Pat would need more time. Interviewing Tony and the CSI people took most of the day. Officer Bara gave his approval for the next morning, allowing them entrance into the evidence room on their own. Captain Saunders had set up a meeting with all of his department detectives involved with both double homicides. Kelsey would be available by phone for questions from his hospital bed. Captain Sean Saunders was beginning to feel some pressure from above.

*****

"Come on, Abron, where's your grit?" questioned Scott. Abron's rehab trainer was trying a touch of mental pressure to get the most out of his charge. Abron was finally free of his headgear three weeks ahead of schedule. Lack of neck movement except for the second attack three weeks earlier had Scott pushing Kelsey, albeit slowly, to regain better side-to-side and up/down movement of his head. Abron's abdominal wound had healed fast enough to allow him to work on physical training for his shoulders and legs. The hand and head holes had healed enough to where the wounds were closed. "We can't get to heavy with your midsection yet. Slow stationary bicycling for no more than ten minutes a day will have to do for the next week. Don't blow it and jump the gun. Keep it slow and steady." Scott was a former police officer from Walla Walla. "I was injured on the job," he answered Abron. Officer Kelsey was curious about how Scott became interested in physical therapy. "Being injured in a high-speed chase, while in service, pretty much changed things for me in an instant. I did get lucky though when my rehab boss ended up my wife."

"That says it all," replied Abron. "How long was your therapy? And schooling?" he asked.

"Thanks to Julie, a career change morphed into reality. The schooling took a while but was worth the fight. The job affords me more time off and the freedom of movement. I do a lot of work with clients in their home. How about you? Married?"

Abron said, "Never have been. Marine corps then college. Haven't had the time. There is a POI for the first time. Here name is Isabel."

"Izzy?" Scott replied. Seeing the look of astonishment on Abron's face painted a picture, forcing Scott to do some fast background history. "Short blond hair, keen mind, and in-charge attitude?"

To which Abron replied, "I guess she gets around."

"No, no, no, Abron, she is a great young lady. I met her when she was just thirteen years old and in rehab with me. Izzy was there because of a skiing accident. Did you know, she was being touted as an aspiring Olympic hopeful in downhill and slalom? Isabel had won or placed in just about every major junior competition throughout the Northwest. Her injury was so severe it took three or four operations on her hip and leg to put her back together again. Her competitive skiing was over. Julie and I enjoy talking to her now and again at the Davenport Hotel, downtown. Did you know she's back to bartending, on crutches?"

"I think she told me about the Davenport gig, but at the time, I was pretty foggy due to my incident. I heard she's graduating from Cheney. Do you know where and when?" Abron asked. Before Scott could answer, Deputy Kelsey came clean. "Isabel has a hold of me. My mom always said when it hits me, it would be like a freight train. Up to my career in the Marine corps, I had never brought a lady home to meet her. I think they began to worry this only child wouldn't produce grandkids."

Scott answered with an invitation. "Be our guest. I'll have Julie call you a week ahead of time. She'll make sure we're next to the Davis clan. Where are your parents living, Abron?"

"Retired and living up in Charleston, Oregon. It's a suburb of Coos Bay. My dad's a retired aerospace engineer. Mom was a teacher. They spend most of their time catching Dungeness crab, clamming, and fishing for salmon. Mom has a blackberry, raspberry, huckleberry garden that would amaze you."

"I've never eaten Dungeness," remarked Scott. "How does it compare with king?"

"Sweeter, but a lot of work. They're small, requiring a lot of digging to get a mouthful."

"I'd like to try it sometime," replied Scott.

Abron added, "It's tastier fresh out of the bay. Maybe we could visit my folks someday. Dad and I drop the pots in the morning and collect them just before dinner. He owns a beautiful twenty-four-foot all-weather moored at the arena."

"As you first said, where and when?" answered Scott.

*****

That afternoon

"Dr. Marsh and Scott seem to be hinting at something. And now you? Is there something more than you're letting on?"

Izzy replied, "I can't let the cat out of the bag. I shouldn't have said anything. You caught me overwhelmed by your amazing recuperation. Then Scott's comment just now—oops, I almost did it again." Changing the subject faster than Abron could keep up with, she added, "Someday soon I'd like to go on that dinner date you promised me. I don't mean to be pushy, but one of us has to force the issue."

"Issue?" Abron said. "Izzy, I don't understand. What issue?"

"Us," she said again with a smile.

The following day found Abron and Scott at it again. "Can we jog today?" asked Abron.

Scott answered, "We've been pushing your rehab faster than I normally do with patients. You seem to have a tremendous ability to fight through pain and the monotony of repetition." Scott added further, "Tomorrow we'll talk about stepping up your regimen."

Abron had a look of confusion and apprehension. "Am I healing inside? The migraines are less painful but not totally subsiding. At times I still have some pretty bad abdominal pains that make it difficult to do sit-ups. I'm afraid I'll tear something."

Scott jumped in. "Dr. Marsh is coming to see you as we speak. I can't tell you more. That part of your wellness is your doctor's concern. I'm to wait for their okay to begin pushing you even harder." Scott's cell phone rang, and he picked up. "That's a good thing. I'll be right there. Abron, we're cutting this session a few minutes short. You have a visitor. I'll see you tomorrow afternoon."

This time Isabel walked in with a swagger—no crutches, her leg in a walking cast, and a smile that seemed to show she was exceptionally glad to be where she was at that moment. "Feeling better or worse after your rehab session?" Isabel questioned.

"One hundred percent now that you're here," Abron replied. "And look at you, no crutches. Does it hurt to walk or stand?"

"Better every day," she replied.

"Well then, would you like that ski lesson now?" asked Abron.

Isabel tried to control her laughter and emotions. Isabel replied, "Scott told me the good news. It looks like I may take you up on that although it will have to be next winter. My neighbor told me Schweitzer Basin and 49 degrees are shutting down in two or three weeks. The old Jackass ski area in Kellogg may stay open until the end of the month, if there's a lucky late-season snow. With your injuries, I would think we're doomed to spend the summer picnicking and harvesting huckleberries." Izzy then said mischievously, "I know you know, Abron! Dr. Marsh told me he hadn't given you the go-ahead. But somehow you figured it out." Abron was giving her a sly look. "Dr. Paul wanted me to be the one to tell you it's time to go home. I also want to be the one that picks you up at your apartment for a dinner date tomorrow night. Dad and Mom are going to drive us. They said they wanted to keep an eye on you."

Later that evening, after Izzy went home, Abron met with Dr. Marsh and Scott. "We're going to give you a little R & R from the hospital and rehab," said Dr. Paul (as Abron referred to Marsh). "You're being released tonight. Officer Pat Price is going to escort you back to your residence after we take out all the remaining stitches and staples." The doctor winked at

Abron. "But you already knew that, if Isabel did her job. Scott will continue with in-home rehab five days a week for a while. We've scheduled several checkups and x-ray sessions for you over the next six weeks. Since you've turned away our attempts at painkillers and most other meds, I'm prescribing a healthy regime of vitamins. Take them seriously. Your bones and veins could use some backup. Keep your physical activities at a safe level. Listen to Scott. He's worked up a schedule to put you back at your desk soon. Do not drive for the next few weeks or until I clear you. We're still mildly concerned about a blackout from your concussion and headaches. I've notified Captain Saunders. You'll soon be available to begin light duty. Take it slowly, and you'll be just fine. The concussion and broken verte-brae will haunt you for a while, but time will heal. I'll see you in a few days."

Scott then coordinated his home visits. And then he, too, departed and left Abron to check out.

The next evening, Abron's doorbell rang. Isabel was happy with what she found when he opened the door. Her six-foot-three-inch hunk was standing, clothed and smiling, like the night he had asked for coffee out at the Bump Inn. Abron got a warm lingering hug from Izzy. "They won't let me drive yet," he opened. "Could I lean on you to get us to our first date?" he asked, with an air of excitement. "I really wanted this to be our second or maybe fifth date before spring. But then injuries got in the way. Hope I'm not too forward?"

"Don't push your luck" came the reply. With her eyes wide and a seductive smile capturing his full attention, Isabel put her arms carefully back around Abron and whispered softly, "Deputy Kelsey, you're paying the bill and putting gas in my car. Remember, I'm just a helpless, starving student." Izzy's mischievous look came out again. Abron was immediately and helplessly turned into a smitten man, in love for the first time. Hand in hand, they headed for Izzy's mom and dad waiting in the car.

*****

*Captain Saunders's office. Spokane,
Washington. Early spring.*

"We need some answers," ordered Captain Saunders. "Dead bodies on both sides of the state line. Presumed torture in both cases. Disappearing witnesses. Our own deputy attacked and almost murdered, twice. A stone-cold crime scene igniting under our noses. The facts are glaring at us. But we're not putting two and two together. The same MO was defined at each of the homicide locations. Ron, I want you to get together with Lieutenant Tony Bara from CDA sheriff's. The two of you need to figure out how to rattle more cages.

"Our DA and I requested FBI intervention using proof of unionized labor involvement. When homicides or kidnapping are involved, especially across state lines, it's a given the FBI will intervene eventually. Our district attorney and assistant DA, Cynthia Berdot, are both communicating with our office daily. Not in a good way. Pat and Terry, we need more detectives. Report to me, in twenty-four hours, with your recommendations on the best-qualified officers from our street division. We need more eyes, ears, and feet on the ground working these cases. The heat is on."

The next morning, Captain Saunders was given the names of six potential detectives within their organization. All six were given "battlefield" promotions. That afternoon, the six detectives were paired and briefed. Most of their work would be made up of long hours interviewing neighbors and friends of the McCoys and Nelsons. His priority leaned to the high-profile McCoy case. Four deputy investigators were assigned to Lieutenant Jake Monroe. Terry, Ron, and Pat took the remainder under their wings. Saunders knew he needed hundreds, if not thousands, of hours spent door-to-door.

✻✻✻✻✻

San Bernardino Sheriff's Office, California

Sergeant Mike Gwen loved history. For him, TV viewing was the History channel, National Geographic, PBS, and Turner classic movies. He and his family were now residing in Highlands, California. Staying in communication with his deputy buddies up in Spokane was made much easier with the advent of the internet. All six officers of the original Bump Inn society tossed pleasantries and insults back and forth almost nightly. Mike always returned the sarcasm. Recently, Sergeant Gwen was given a case involving two gold coins turned over to the district attorney's office in San Bernardino. Not just any gold coins. Individually, their value exceeded $600,000. The pawnshop broker had paid out less than $10,000 for both rare coins. The sellers were "shady characters." The buyer did the best he could in describing them: "They wore sunglasses, baseball hats, blue jeans, and were in a hurry." They had told the broker they had tickets to the Dodger game in Los Angeles. The owner of the pawn store knew the value and called the police the moment they were out the door. In-store cameras had filmed their presence at the counter front.

When Gwen interviewed the buyer, he came away with several important and lucky facts on the POIs, other than the descriptions corroborated by the camera footage. "Obviously," the buyer told Gwen, "they were desperate for money and hadn't a clue of the real value of the 1854-O Liberty Head coins. One recently sold for almost $600,000 at auction."

Gwen asked, "Why did you buy them knowing they were probably hot?"

The buyer's answer was honest and surprised Gwen but made perfect sense coming from a business-man. "I'm hoping the reward will be more substantial than my initial investment. Someone is missing them." Gwen was mystified that the case had landed in his lap just after his taking the job in San Bernardino. He questioned the pawnshop owner on the persons of interest's ages, demeanors, and clothing, asking if they said anything more that he thought could be a clue as to why they were in his new city. He couldn't wait to send the information on to Spokane after an okay was given by his own boss.

That night, Officer Gwen was emailing the message to all five of his buds and his former captain. "Something of interest has come up." He explained the coins and their values then added two head-scratchers. "The sellers wore baseball caps—one was a Spokane Flyers hat, the other a Nelson, BC, hockey hat! Second point of interest: the History channel recently ran a piece on a train robbery out of Butte, Montana, that took place back in the 1890s. It mentioned there were several hundred of these newly minted gold coins that had been jacked. The documentary also noted other items stolen from the same train car, including opium, laudanum, and several hundred pounds of unrefined gold nuggets. FYI, Rose Lake."

*****

The next evening, Spokane deputies were gathered around a table at the Bump. Lieutenant Tony Bara, from the Idaho Sheriff's Office, and his captain, Terry Croop, joined them. After introductions, Bara said, "I've filled Chief Croop in on those coins found by your former Sergeant Gwen. The value is staggering." Tony turned it over to his Captain.

She began, "If those coins came from our area? Murder, kidnapping, and all sorts of mayhem could be associated with whomever knows about them or possesses them. Lieutenant Bara will handle the task of researching the validity of their existence. Tony will be working with two professors of northwest history—one from Gonzaga and the other from University of Montana out of Missoula. A meeting has been set for the first of next week. Tony has been advised to share all info with your office in Spokane. It's the best motive/lead we have had to date, but first we need proof of their existence and where they came from."

"May we talk to the professors directly?" asked Ron Rowe.

"Only in an emergency," June replied. "Professor John Laskowski is at Gonzaga, Bob Wood at the University of Montana. Both are in midterm, and their time spent comes through homework after classes. Tony has their numbers and hours available. Before I leave, your captain, Saunders, filled me in yesterday on the aluminum foundry leads your office is on top of. Please inform me directly if they, in anyway, breach our shared border. Thank you, detectives," Croop said as she departed.

For Ron, Terry, and Pat the investigation was finally producing creditable leads. Abron would be notified that night via email. When Abron received the email, a question jumped out immediately: "Why did it take two years and my near death to pressure the CDA Sheriff Department into action?"

Even though Abron and Christian had been to the Nelsons once before without interruptions, this visit would possibly provide a greater understanding of what took place inside the barn. On his way to Rose Lake, Abron was apprehensive. His last trip on duty with the sheriff's department had ended in a personal injury nightmare. After four months of rehab, Abron felt he could take care of himself in most situations, though he still had some reservations.

"Christian, this doesn't feel normal. I'm okay except that the memory of the day you saved me is still not clear."

Christian replied, "First trip out, we were going to explore the buildings and maybe take a walk around the perimeter of the farm. You've had a chance to study the case files. I hope they cleared up some of your conceptions. I'm thinking this time out could jog your memory. Hopefully we'll find something useful." Deputy Caine recognized Kelsey's apprehension. He knew Abron needed some nudging. "When we get there, let's start with a walkabout."

As they pulled up to the farmhouse, sitting in plain sight was an older white Ford pickup parked between the house and the barn. Christian approached the front door with gun drawn; Abron was standing behind the open car door facing the front porch. Christian knocked then announced loudly "Sheriff. Open the door."

An older man came around the corner on the north side of the house. "What the hell, guys?"

"Is this your truck?" asked Christian.

"Yes, it is. I'm a neighbor from about a mile down the road south of here. Name's Elliot, Elliot Carlson."

Christian holstered his weapon while Abron stepped from behind the car door. Both officers' minds were beginning to calm. "Sorry about the weapons drawn, Mr. Carlson, but we're both a little jumpy. The last time we were here my partner, Abron here, almost lost his life."

"I remember it well," answered Elliot. "The start of winter. Heard we almost lost you."

Abron said, "I don't remember much about that day. The place was supposed to be vacant. I've been told my partner saved my life?"

"Did you get a look at the bastards?" asked Carlson.

"I wish, but the day's a complete blank." Abron questioned Elliot, "What brought you here?"

"I've been hired by the inheriting relatives to check for break-ins or water running, anything that could damage the buildings."

"Why now?" queried Abron.

"This is my twenty-eighth month of checking the property. I didn't start yesterday," Elliot replied.

"There's no mention of you in any of the reports covering this place. I'm wondering why?" asked Kelsey.

"I guess because no one ever talked to me. I don't feel I have to chase law enforcement down to give a statement. Especially since everybody in North Idaho has been talked to except me. I've wanted to give a statement or, in my case, blow the whistle on Joe and Wesley Nelson since this whole mess started. But law enforcement doesn't think I'm worth talking to."

"Can our detectives talk to you?" asked Abron.

"I hope it won't take another two years. When can this happen?" Elliot asked.

"As soon as we can make it back to the office. Detectives Ron Rowe and Sal Domenico will want to give you a call tonight or tomorrow morning."

Elliot replied, "Look forward to it. My notes on the Nelsons are about twenty pages thick. But for now, I'll mosey down the road. My cows need milking."

Abron's phone vibrated. "It's Saunders. He wants us back at the station by four p.m. Says it's important. That gives us a two-hour window to have a look around," said Abron.

Four locks kept everyone out of the barn and two storage sheds. All had been put there by the CDA Sheriff's Department. The locks shared the same key. Christian spoke first. "The barn and sheds have been worked over by everybody and their mothers, according to the reports. Virtually nothing has been reported about the house. Since our time is limited again today, why don't we take a quick walk through the house?"

Their first discovery was that the Nelsons kept a neat place. Checking upstairs and down, everything had a place. It was Christian who noticed the many bookshelves in the den. "Joe and Wesley were readers," he pointed out. "*Mysteries of the Northwest, Northwest History*, recipe books. Even prospecting and mining books. Look at this grouping, Abron, 'treasure hunting sites of Idaho and Montana,' 'techniques of underground dynamiting.' And of course, a section on fishing and gardening."

"I thought both Nelsons were employed by our aluminum foundry," commented Kelsey.

"Wesley had gone back to school at North Idaho after just eight or nine months on the job. He worked under his dad as a truck driver for the foundry."

Abron then stated, "For a couple of bachelors, they have a lot of knickknacks collecting dust."

Christian gave a nod and said, "We need to get back to the station for that meeting with Saunders. It'll take us at least an hour-and-a-half drive time."

When they were inside the car headed out the long dirt driveway, Caine asked, "Did you spot any of the surveillance hidden in figurines and light fixtures?"

"After spotting the one in the corner of the front porch overhang, I couldn't help but notice several inside."

"Were they live?" asked Christian. "We both played it well. I'm 90 percent sure we were being watched. I also found some listening devices."

"We need our CSI unit to go through the house."

Christian replied, "Let's drop a report on Cap's desk and let him decide the best route to take." Heading for the Fourth of July pass, both agreed that interviewing Elliot would be interesting, to say the least.

*****

Terry Hollander introduced the officers to Elliot Carlson. Elliot's property included eighty acres of open grass surrounded by beautiful wooded flat land. The southern border butted up to Killarney Lake where Elliot had built a small dock. His fourteen-foot aluminum boat and motor were tied up to the pilings, ready for easy access.

"Elliot," said Ron Rowe, "I know it's been over two years since the murders up the road. I understand you were never interviewed. Let's start with the day of the murders. Was there anything unusual? Maybe noises, action on the highway? Anything at all you thought was out of the daily norm?"

"Let me ask you this first, sheriff. Have you talked with Cora and Dan Snider? The Nelsons' neighbors to the north?"

Lieutenant Tony Bara responded, "Our CDA detectives did but came away with nothing useful."

"Bullshit," responded Elliot. "It's pretty obvious to me that none of your people got to first base with the Sniders!" Everyone quickly woke up. Elliot commanded their attention. "The Sniders and the Nelsons were in a bitter feud. There were dog poisonings, broken windows. The Sniders even tried to take some of the Nelsons' property by claiming a boundary access road belonged to Cora and Dan. That dirt road was completely on the Nelsons' property. The Sniders were using it to access their hayfield behind the house. They were warned to stay off by Joe Nelson. They ignored it until Joe threw nails up and down the supposed easement. Just after that is when the fire started."

"Fire?" said Bara.

"Oh, you missed that one too. It was in the stand-alone garage next to the house. The Nelsons rebuilt that barn in a week and added security cameras at the entrances. The repair was handled quickly, like it never happened. The whole mess seemed fishy to me."

"The fire was never reported. How did you come by all this information?" Lieutenant Bara asked, embarrassingly.

"I don't have a clear line of sight from my house, but I spend a lot of hours in that boat out on the water when it's not frozen over. That was a mild winter. It's amazing what you can see with a good set of binoculars and some fishing time on your hands. If you'll take a moment to step on board, I'll show you something important."

All four were in the boat when Elliot took an unexpected turn to the north through some cattails and reeds. In seconds they had traveled about fifty or sixty feet when a small waterway opened up in front of them. Fifteen- to twenty-feet wide, the water lane ran through a stand of jack pines. All four men were now staring at both the Nelsons' and Sniders' backyards. "The crappie fishing is great on this canal in the spring and fall. The canal system was built by logging and mining companies back around the turn of the century. It once linked all these lakes into Coeur d'Alene Lake. You can kind of picture how it made transporting logs and minerals up to CDA doable. As far as I know, none of my neighbors ever used the canal for anything."

Back on solid ground, Lieutenant Bara reiterated, "There was never a word of this mentioned in any of our reports. I think we all see why. The Sniders wouldn't volunteer any of that information. The spotlight would shine on them immediately as POIs."

"Lieutenant," Ron interrupted, "may Terry and I question the Sniders?"

"If you'll take our Officer Flores with," he replied.

"Elliot," asked Ron, "are the Sniders large people?"

"No, Dan's about my height, Cora maybe five feet, three inches and thin."

Detective Rowe furthered, "Do the Sniders have any adult kids or relatives that you've noticed visiting or living there?"

"I've met their only sons, twins, Al and Arnie. Good kids. They live over in Libby, Montana. Both work for the forest service."

Ron continued, "At the time of the murders, had you noticed any strange vehicles during the day or night—vans or light trucks?"

Elliot scratched his chin, thought for a few seconds, and then answered, "Except for the occasional visits by law enforcement, there wasn't much traffic out on the highway. As I said before, I have a poor line of sight from my house to the roadway and the Nelsons' house"—pointing in the direction of the road—"I did notice some type of repair going on at the Sniders' a couple of months before the murders. Pickup trucks, nothing heavy. The outfit they hired rolled a portable cement mixer and generator on to the property. The job was completed in less than three weeks."

"Can you remember the name of the construction company?" asked Terry.

"Yes, I took a card from them, just in case I needed help that summer. I tossed it after I called them to give me a bid on a job. They were no longer in business. I called the BBB, thinking maybe they moved, but they had no listing either. You might want to ask the Sniders?"

Terry finished the interview with a couple of departing questions. "How long have you been living here, Elliot?"

"Over ten years."

"What kind of work did you do up to retirement?"

"I worked for Hecla Mining out of Kellogg and Wallace. Underground mostly and always gyppo."

When Terry and Ron were back in the car riding to Spokane, Terry brought it up first even though both investigators had been thinking about it. "Elliot steered the questions away from himself and never asked us to enter his house."

Ron added, "For two or three cows and no other livestock I could see, Elliot has a barn big enough to hold a rodeo. We don't know if he has family or much else. He's going to need some follow-up."

"Spokane sheriff's dispatch, can I take a message?"

"This is Captain Link Mathis over in Superior, Montana. Is Detective Terry Hollander available?"

"Yes, one moment."

"Terry Hollander."

"Terry, this is Link Mathis. You might remember me from our old days in a squad car chasing and catching, I might add, a stolen truck at De Borgia?"

"Yes, Link, man, it's been seven or eight years since that excitement. I still can't believe we stopped him with only a squad car and some flares."

"Terry, I know your boss, but I don't want to bother him at an early stage. I think you'll see why. Our boys might have located the Ford truck you're looking for!"

"If you did, we and the CDA Sheriff's Department would breathe a lot easier. The pressure has been on and getting hotter as we speak."

Link asked, "How do you want to handle this?"

"Is there a flight risk, Link?"

"Truck's been in and out for several days but seems to be stationary now with a flat tire."

"This could be a monster break. Let me hit our captain over the head with this. Can you hold the line for a minute?"

After a moment's pause there came "Link Mathias, the last time I saw you, I was ducking your fore on the 11th fairway in Missoula."

Link replied, "Too much fun. Law enforcement should stay in law enforcement. You healthy, Sean?"

"Me? If I remember, you're the old-timer!"

With a laugh, Link fired back, "Three days difference, and you've been married twice. That's got to cost you at least a year in aging."

"Link Mathis, let's get together after all this is over and talk old times."

"If you'll include Terry, I'm in. Terry tell you what we've found?"

To which Sean replied, "We've already got our fingers crossed."

"Could use an extra hand or two for surveillance over here. We're sure we found your Ford truck and persons of interest just outside of Superior. I've got two sets of eyes on them. They haven't made us. I understand this to be a murder investigation, so we're laying low. Our guys have been instructed not lose the truck or either perp no matter what. We're stretched thin over here due to budget cuts."

"When, how many, and where can they report?" said Sean.

Link replied, "I've personally got eyes on them at this time, and the surveillance is covered through the next couple of days. But we could use some relief after the weekend."

*****

Spring had arrived in the Northwest. There was still a chance of a late snowfall or two. Terry, Ron, Christian, Jake, Sal, and now Maria and Tony Bara from CDA were back in their corner of the Bump. Tony wanted to be a part of the entire picture since the Newman lake and Rose Lake incidents could be connected. However, tonight most of the talk was about Neuman Lake, helping Tony and Maria better understand the McCoy homicides. Abron pulled into the parking lot a little after six, just getting off a ten-hour shift in Montana watching the two men that drove the white Ford pickup. Ron asked, "Anything worth shouting about on the POIs?"

"I followed them back into Idaho as far as the turn to St. Maries. Same result that Link told us about with his crew. They seem to vanish when they turn south. I scoured the roads for any signs around the Nelsons' place to no avail. We need to coordinate a second and third relay to follow them after the St. Maries cutoff. I-90 is straight enough at times, where the perps can easily spot us if we get any closer than a mile behind."

"They have an interest in the Rose and Killarney Lake areas. At least that's what it seems," said Terry and furthered, "Maybe Tony and his team can fill in the gap?"

"Are you on tomorrow?" asked Tony.

"Eight a.m. until closing," Abron replied. "I'll coordinate a hand off at the I-90 junction with another car two miles and a third four miles south."

"Call me when they make a move tomorrow. We'll be ready," offered Tony.

Ron Rowe jumped into the conversation. "Terry asked me to give some factual input on the findings to date. They could help link both double homicides. I think you'll recognize the relevance in what I have for you." Ron began. "Over the last four years, there have been three upper-level union bosses who have moved away from North Idaho. All were living within a fifty-mile radius of Rose Lake. Does it seem like a coincidence or a strong lead? Two double murders, illegal payouts, union and company corruption. Graft all the way down to laymen that worked within the aluminum plant.

"The Nelsons both worked, at one time or another, for the union. Our former assistant DA prosecuted both union employees and the corporation. Then add to the pot, David McCoy's tie-in to the Nelsons. He had defended them in court on a separate civil matter."

"Can we get the names of the higher-ups gone missing?" asked Maria.

"I'll email names and new addresses later tonight," said Ron.

The hour was late; the group decided to end the meeting for a couple of days. This would afford them time to develop questions that could lead both sides of the border to a better understanding of the entirety of the cases. Tony and Maria left together in the same unmarked car. While not unusual, the departure didn't go unnoticed.

*****

Saunders couldn't believe the gold mine of information he was handed by the DA. He read into the early morning hours. Saunders got to work early, and by 8:00 a.m., several meetings were scheduled for his department heads. Abron Kelsey had a note on his desk to see the captain immediately before the meetings were to begin.

"Captain."

Saunders looked up and answered, "Abron, I've been going over your education information. We need to utilize your legal knowledge in our investigations of both double homicides. How much further is your journey to the state bar exam?"

Kelsey was immediately wide-awake. "Sir, I enjoy coming to work as a forensics specialist. The law degree was secondary to what I'm trained for and interested in."

Captain Saunders said, "Answer the question."

"I would be qualified and ready for the bar by November."

"This is not a demotion nor a promotion," replied the captain. "Right now, I need your expertise of state and federal laws pertaining to our investigations into the Newman and, now, Rose Lake murders. There are state lines being crossed. Jurisdictions are tricky from state to state. I think you're in the right place at the right time for this department. You'll be teamed with Rowe for the Superior stakeout.

"I'm also going to send you to FBI headquarters in Chicago next month. The DA's office feels they need you to present our cases in person. We'll talk more about that later. We need to get to my eight o'clock. Officer Kelsey, everything we've discussed stays between you and I. Ron and yourself will be a part of the second meeting scheduled for ten. At that time, you'll better understand the importance of the new assignment."

"Aye, Captain."

As Abron turned to leave, Saunders caught him off guard by asking, "I don't mean to pry into your private life, but are you and Isabel an item yet?"

Confused, Abron answered, "I have a dinner date with Izzy tonight."

"We may also need her education before this case is sent to the DA. I understand she is majoring in sociology, with a secondary interest in Northwest history. I took the liberty of talking with one of her counselors out at Cheney. He told me her career interest was swaying toward criminology. At this point in time, that part of her studies is not relevant.

"Isabel's Northwest history classes have come into play with Tony Bara's professors, Laskowski and Woods. Casually talk to her about the 1890s train robbery over in Butte. See if she would be interested in working with the DA's office, part-time. She would act as our eyes and ears with both professors. Isabel's counselor claims she has a brilliant mind for detail. I think it's worth a shot if she can find the time in her schedule. None of this is written in concrete, but keep it in mind. We're going to need every resource we can muster. See you at today's meetings."

Abron agreed to talk to Isabel on the QT.

Abron and Ron entered the conference room on time with pencils and notepads in hand. It was a surprise to see the number of people seated and standing. Captain Sanders was behind a podium at the far end of the room. Introductions included representatives from the DA's office, Coeur d'Alene DA, plus sheriff's deputies from Washington, Idaho, and Montana. Two suits from the FBI and several other unidentified persons, looking official, were also present. There were no smiles in the room. Terry Hollander recognized the aluminum plant union representative standing with a gray-haired gentleman sporting a name tag, identifying him as a company man, from the factory.

Surprisingly, the feds were first to speak. The presentation was well prepared and included information kits to all persons attending this closed meeting. The FBI information caught almost everyone off guard. Their report was the main reason for the meeting. It was an amazing presentation basically showcasing three years of investigation that touched seventeen states across America. The FBI presented a story of local greed and corruption between union workers and company officials. The corporation and union being focused on this morning belonged to the Spokane area. The FBI's spokesperson presented an array of illegalities connected to local investigations.

The union and company had conspired to hide dirty water laced with cyanide and other carcinogens over the past ten years. The illegal dumping, interstate transfer of materials, and defiling of federal land and waterways were bought and paid for in a collusion between union and company. The union was laced with mob ties. The payoffs, over the years, totaled several million dollars and involved no less than a dozen company employees and union members. Jail time was imminent. Another bombshell exploded when an agreement between the company and the feds was divulged as already in place—sixty million dollars toward cleanup and legal fees. All in the room were shocked that this took place without their knowledge. Captain Saunders, through all of this, noted there was never a whisper of murder in the report.

The Spokane DA's Office was up next. Basically, names of persons and indictments were divulged along with charges filed against persons living in Washington, Idaho, and Montana. When the meeting came to an end, there were more questions than answers for both DA representatives. The bulk of the questions were coming from the combined sheriff teams. The FBI closed the meeting. "Our investigation has been long, tireless, and thorough. It includes persons of interest from federal and state governments, forestry officials, the EPA, three state senators, and those aforementioned union and factory workers. These national and state investigations are still being pursued as we speak. The who, what, where, when, and whys will soon be sent to each of your departments. We believe this information may also help with your past and recent double homicide investigations. The Bureau has assigned several agents to our Spokane office that will assist law enforcement in any way we can. Keep in mind we have not spent taxpayer dollars on your murder investigations. That ball is in each of your corners."

*****

When Abron entered his third meeting of the morning, most of the participants were already seated. Kelsey's new partner, Sergeant Ron Rowe, was seated next to Deputy Pat Price. Like Abron, Pat was new to the job. Price had more seniority than Kelsey, having worked as a deputy for almost two years. Price had never been married, though he was known to have several girlfriends over his short time with the sheriff's department. He loved his job. Being the shortest officer on duty, he was powerfully built and extremely quick when it came time for action. The two deputies had great respect for each other. They knew they could work together and were good with the idea of teaming up.

A Montana sheriff's deputy was first to speak. "We have identified the perps under surveillance outside of Superior and are fairly certain they were the two that attacked Abron Kelsey over in Rose Lake. Unfortunately, or fortunately, the Spokane Sheriff's Department will no longer be needed to help with surveillance." A silence fell over the room. All ears were alive. "We have received new input from California—corroborated information from your former Deputy Gwen out of San Bernardino, California. Both perps were gunned down in that county earlier this morning." A murmur grew in intensity.

"They must have flown out of Missoula sometime yesterday morning. Our photos and fingerprinting matched. However, Deputy Gwen has a third person that is connected to our dead perps. He was seen at the pawnshop and later at a local restaurant with the deceased. The images are not sharp enough for our people to run through our system for a match. We have that third person pictured from several different angles at two different locations. His hat and sunglasses always shade his identity. His movements, caught in black-and-white, don't give us much either. He's 5'5" to 5'6", weight 140 to 150, age near 60. As you'll discover, he may have been wearing a phony mustache and wig at both locations. Captain Saunders should receive a more thorough file from San Bernardino any minute. Our Montana surveillance team is taking a back seat at this time. The Superior branch will assist you from here."

*****

Captain Saunders checked his email. When he opened up his .com, all came to light. Sergeant Gwen had not only identified the bodies but, within hours of the shootings in San Bernardino, had also emailed almost thirty pages to his comrades in Spokane. The information package included names, known addresses, phone numbers, and current pictures of all involved. Little was known about the third POI. The information only included rap sheets on the two deceased. A hotline was now in place to all agencies concerned with the six murders.

Late that afternoon, Captain Saunders again gathered his team for update and plan of attack. Captain Saunders made sure no other agencies were involved during the late-afternoon team meeting. Present were Deputies Hollander, Rowe, Price, Kelsey, Caine, and the new detectives Domenico and Monroe. Saunders opened the meeting with a report from the crime lab concerning evidence found at Newman Lake. "Two of our perps left blood splatters at the scene. Neither of which were our POIs killed in San Bernardino. A third person was identified through a piece of skin tissue. The FBI got a hit on it through their national registry. Bryce McCallen, a union rep., we just learned of from the Bureau. He's an associate of Bob Balicki. Looks like they both worked in Chicago around the same period. Both have been lurking in the shadows of our investigations. We need to keep our eyes and ears open for these guys. We can't arrest either one yet. Our friends at the FBI have asked us not to. The Bureau is keeping us abreast of their movements.

"What most of us were prone to believe—both doubles were somehow linked—is still in play but not so matter-of-fact. Our investigation now is into a triple-double. The questions I need answered ASAP: why does a union rep. from out of state have DNA at our Newman Lake crime scene, albeit not in the same time frame of the murders? The minute piece of skin was left at our crime scene several days or weeks before the murders. Where is the link between union and labor at the plant that shows someone was out to get the McCoys? Terry and Ron, we have a change of plans. I want all persons working at the plant over the last five years to be interviewed. Come up with a standard set of questions. When I clear the questions, I want everybody in our building asking them.

"Pat, find out more of the association between the McCoys and Nelsons. Start with that scholarship organization for high school kids. Four of our deceased were involved. Scholarships take money. Were the Nelsons part of the funding? We now have two new union persons of interest linked to Newman Lake. Today we begin the interviews."

*****

The following morning in Spokane

Detectives assigned to the Newman Lake homicides gathered in the main conference room. Captain Saunders asked assistant DA Cynthia Berdot and Gus Taylor, the retired CEO of the aluminum plant, to join them. After introductions, Captain Saunders began with "To better understand what we're facing at Newman Lake, I've asked Cynthia and Gus to give us their insights and concerns. Both have different views of the homicides—Gus from the inside workings of the plant, Cynthia from the DA's office. Ms. Berdot, you have our deputies' attention."

Cynthia began, "The McCoys were a loving couple with several children that had left the nest to start families of their own. Grandchildren are involved, and both sets of the McCoy parents are still living. I tell you this to give more insight into the depth of the DA's interest to want—I should say *demand*—to bring their killers in front of a jury.

"Here's what we know to be true. Robert 'Bob' Balicki has been tied to all six of our murder victims— Nelsons, McCoys, and our two men killed in San Bernardino. Balicki has worked as a union head and liaison to their headquarters in Chicago for the past five years. Within that time, he has averaged six trips per year to Chicago. Using information from the FBI's presentation to all of us, our staff put together a general timeline of his activities and whereabouts when each of the murders were taking place. Please note his forays to Chicago coincide with the homicides. He has the perfect alibi on all three occasions—plane tickets, hotel stays, and phone calls.

"Thanks to the FBI, we know he has a close assistant, Bryce McCallen. The union payoffs to the EPA in our region as well as union graft to a factory head and at least two department foremen within the plant have been established. All are on a 'No touch' list for our law enforcement agencies, courtesy of the FBI. Phyllis McCoy, we believe, was beginning to make people nervous. The DA's office was following a course of prosecution against Balicki, McCallen, and the union itself, spearheaded by Phyllis. Obviously on hold, for now. I will be in charge of carrying that investigation to conclusion.

"FYI, we also have learned that David McCoy represented Mr. Balicki in a felony trial that goes back almost five years. Bob went free but not before spending five figures on his own defense. The link between Balicki and McCallen, with the Nelsons, is definitively union through workplace. As you know, Joe was tortured at Rose Lake. Did Joe have something on Balicki? We believe the assassins in all three cases, along with Officer Kelsey's attack, came from the union under outside orders. Gus Taylor has something you should know."

Gus Taylor had just recently turned eighty. He walked slow and acted the part of a retired CEO. When he spoke, however, Gus was exact and to the point. "I did not take a plea bargain to remain free. The Bureau and our own DA's office cleared my name. I do believe Assistant DA Berdot is telling you the truth concerning the union in our state. I would like to add the following to what she has given you. The deceased person that tried a second attempt on Officer Kelsey's life and wounded another officer outside Kelsey's room previously worked for the aluminum factory. We located and identified him through a copy of his driver's license.

"Fortunately, one of the company's corporate laws makes the local factory keep this information on hand for seven years. There were two Chavez brothers that worked at the plant. Both also worked in the timber and mining industries over in North Idaho. I've given your captain my cell and home phone numbers. In my retirement, I spend most days out at Athol, working on and flying a tri wing, open cockpit, vintage reproduction. Because of my age, they refer to me at the airport as the Red Baron. I'm easy to find, if needed."

*****

Isabel had taken the part-time job working for Captain Saunders. She wasted no time in her pursuit of what seemed to be lost treasure. By phone, she introduced herself to Professors Laskowski and Wood, later exchanging emails. Within twenty-four hours, the messages came pouring in from their offices at Montana State and Gonzaga. Professor Wood was pro-robbery. He felt all researched information was on the up-and-up. The incident took place; the booty was secreted off.

Professor Laskowski also approved of what they found. "Yes, there was a train robbery." His research, however, cast some doubt as to the validity of the stolen items. "Laudanum in those days came in small glass capsules that wouldn't have survived a pack-animal journey. The amount of heroin taken was laboriously heavy. The robbers probably would not have known what they had or how to distribute it for a profit. Why gold nuggets? The train was departing Butte, not arriving? Butte was the regional processing plant for raw minerals. The nuggets would have been in bar form. The missing gold coins were existent at that time. Hard to believe they could also disappear in time. Too much value." His final comment was "Those cowboys needed to eat."

Isabel began the compilation of information she would later send to Captain Saunders. Using the internet, Izzy Davis ran her own checks on the two professors. She couldn't find what she thought would be available. The bios on both fell far short of allowing her a look into the two elderly scholars. She needed to know which, in her mind, would take the project more seriously. Isabel decided to meet both face-to-face. Montana State would be the longest drive. Add to that Professor Woods passé attitude toward the long-forgotten robbery, and that made him interviewee number 1. A meeting was set for a Sunday two weeks out. Excited to be working with the sheriff's office and the Spokane DA, Isabel went ahead and set up a meeting with the closer Professor Laskowski at Gonzaga the Sunday before her meeting with Woods. Though the meetings were reversed, time would be saved.

*****

Circa late 1800s

The next morning, after the men had gone back to their construction site, Molly and Henry, under the cover of brush and bush, crept down to the campsite. They found the rock structure to be a dry well close to eighteen-feet deep. Henry lit a small amount of scrub grass on fire, dropping it down the hole. No water in sight. Just a mound of mud and dirt with a couple of empty broken and whole whiskey bottles scattered on one side. From the location of the well, the new construction site was not visible. Signs of a used campfire were present about ten feet from the well.

"Who dug it?" Molly asked.

"It's been here for a long while," Henry replied.

"Howdy, strangers" came a voice. "You're a long way from nowhere."

Surprised but stone-faced, Henry replied, "Just passin' through when we saw the wheel ruts headed up this canyon. Thought we'd take a look."

"Me and my partners have been here about a month, looking to spend summers logging these woods," stated the stranger. "The mill should be producing as soon as the boiler gets here. We've been spending most of our time dragging timber. Plan on being here long?" he asked.

Henry lied and said, "Nope, we're headed south to pick up supplies for our home." Then he asked,

"Was there a farm anywhere near? This well is several years old."

"We don't know the history of this meadow, but we did see a couple of grave markers and signs of a log cabin about ten minutes up that draw," replied the stranger.

"I'm Henry, and this is Molly. You got a name?"

"Molly," the stranger shot back, "that's where I've seen you. Don't you own that halfway house up north on the north fork? Me and my partners have stayed there over the last year or so."

Molly didn't answer. Henry noticed and said, "That's her. Thanks for the information. We'll be on our way while we still have some daylight." With no horses or buckboard in sight, Henry and the stranger decided to let things lie.

Henry asked, "Is that wagon path dependable?"

"We used it a few times since we started work. Lot of ruts, but passable."

As the two were trekking toward the west end of the meadow, Molly asked, "Did you see that pile of fresh dirt and rock down in the hole?"

"Something's going on down there. It could be a cave-in from the stone wall or somebody is digging," answered Henry.

The stranger watched them go until they were out of sight then headed back to talk with his pals.

"You thinkin' what I'm thinkin', Henry?"

"Yeah. We'd better keep a keen eye out. That cowboy never told us his name but sure wanted to know our business."

"Let's hide the wagon and do some scouting this evening."

Later that day, around sunset, Henry and Molly were traversing down an adjacent draw that turned into the canyon with the meadow and the men. A large campfire was lighting up the area. Within the ring of light sat three men. Molly spoke first. "Those are the two cowboys that had the map."

"Yeah," said Henry. "And that's the stranger we met this morn. I don't likely remember him visiting the inn, do you?" Molly shook her head no. Henry started making plans. "There sure not straying far from that well. Let's sneak down by those bushes where you'll have a line of fire with that Winchester. I'll move in a little further and try to catch some of their talk. If you see danger coming at us, let loose. I'm confident with this double-barreled shotgun and you covering me, we've got an advantage. There's too much light in their eyes for them to see much past the fire."

As Henry neared, he heard them saying, "I don't like them two dogging us like that. I know for certain that Molly went through our belongings at the inn when we were there. She could have seen the map. With that telegraph line and the railroad passing by, they're sure to know about us robbing the train."

"Are you sure that was Molly and her lackey?"

The third stranger replied, "Your description of them fits."

"Let's trail them tomorrow at daylight, see what they're up to. We don't want any more partners to share the gold."

"Bodies could go missing out here and never be found."

"I'd sure like another go at that Molly before it happens." All three agreed.

When Henry reached Molly, he said, "They're onto us. If I was a bettin' man, I'd say their riches are hidden close by."

Molly replied, "If they aim to do us in, I think they need killin'."

"Right now's the best time, while we can surprise them," said Henry. "You think you can hit them from here?"

To which Molly replied, "I can't miss with the first shot, but the other two birds will be on the fly in a heartbeat."

"This scatter gun will get one, maybe two, just don't miss the first one," said Henry.

"A 200 count should give me time to be in position. Shoot to kill."

As Henry scurried back down to the meadow, Molly found a recent windfall to rest her Winchester on. The view was perfect; the shot not more than two hundred feet, and with the windfall, she would be as steady as a rock. Remembering what Henry said, she counted and squeezed the trigger. The Cowboy facing her direction flew backward off a log, like he had been kicked in the chest by a mule. As the other two jumped up in startled amazement, Henry's shotgun was unloaded on the nearest outlaw. The third Cowboy pulled his .45 and got one shot off before Molly nailed him with a .44 to the chest. When the smoke cleared, Molly could see all three, laying prone in the meadow.

With little light, she took her time getting down to Henry. He was hit in the upper leg. Molly asked, "Is it bad?"

Henry replied, "That jasper hit an artery, Molly. I'm bleeding hard."

"Let's cinch you up, and I'll go for the buggy."

As she stood up, she was thrown straight at Henry; a fourth Cowboy, 'til now unseen, was standing behind Molly with a smoking shotgun.

Henry fired the Colt the same time the stranger let go a second blast from the shotgun. Silence prevailed through the rest of the night.

*****

Their first real date night was to dinner, nothing fancy. The Lodge Pole served above-average entrées. There was home-style cooking with apple, cherry, raspberry, and huckleberry pies to top off the dining. After being seated, Abron began the conversation. "Izzy, I'm not married, never have been. I don't have any kids, and I'm not a murderer."

The surprised look on Isabel's face was as good as a gasp. "You've been talking to Mom and Dad behind my back," she said.

"Your dad hired one of my old cronies from the Marine Corps. I knew he moved to the Spokane area after his enlistment ran out. Lenny started his own intel company named The Eyes Have It. All this was while I was attending the University of Washington. Leonard is a first-class private eye. Leaves no stone unturned. He saw the same headline in the paper about my mishap that you read. When your dad called him, Jack had no idea about Semper Fi. Your mom, dad, and Leonard came to see me in the hospital a couple of days after you first came by. I asked your parents if I could date you when I recuperated. After listening to Leonard, they both gave me the green light."

"I won't apologize," said Isabel. "I'm not looking for a short-term romance, and I didn't want any surprises. Abron, you're the one who should be apologizing to me. I'm self-supporting and about to graduate from college. Did I mention I'm over twenty-one and can speak for myself?"

"Can I still call you Izzy?"

Her smile returned. "Yes."

"Isabel, I'm not a ladies' man. From the first time I saw you at the Bump Inn, you haven't left my thoughts. When I see you, I'm happy. When I hear your voice, my spirits perk up. If I've offended you in any way, I'm deeply sorry. I like you more than any lady I've ever met, with the exception of my mom." He grinned.

The first date went well for both. Isabel held Abron's hand when they departed the restaurant. On the way to her front door, Abron initiated the hand holding. "Good night," he said.

Isabel wasted no time in wrapping her arms around his neck and sensually kissing him. "Goodnight," she said and quickly left him standing in front of the door.

Isabel couldn't believe that a man with so much charm and sincerity could be anything less than the person she wanted to be near. They both were smitten. They both were in the busiest, most-restrictive time for a budding romance. She hoped they would get through the schooling and investigations soon. Isabel, having been contacted by Abron's boss, Captain Saunders, was advised not to mention the call to anyone, at least for a few weeks. He had cautioned her to be observant when she was around Abron. The attempts on his life had not been solved. The value of the twenty-dollar gold pieces could hold the answers.

After their conversation, Izzy had thought long and hard about what she would be getting into. With her busy schedule, she didn't have much time to spare, but the historical value won out. She was ready to jump in with both feet. The bonus would be getting one foot in the door to employment opportunities. Not knowing about covert exploring gave the assignment a fun sense of mystery. She didn't mention the call from Captain Saunders to Abron. Shawn never mentioned to Kelsey the phone conversation. His boss and Isabel would communicate over the net. If she let Kelsey in on her investigation, so be it.

*****

Within days of their first talk, Captain Saunders received a preliminary report from Isabel. It was a basic report on her contact with Professors Wood and Laskowski. The pages included an outline and timeline of the stolen merchandise. A second report would be forthcoming after she met personally with the professors. Izzy supplied him with times, dates, and locations of those meetings, having already been set. *One major question stands out,* he thought. *How do you fence something so valuable?* This was a question Captain Saunders later put to his investigators. Isabel included in that first writing the weight of the gold nuggets, the quantity of laudanum, the 99.9 percent pure heroin, and a gold-coin count. He noted the tie-in to the drug lab found at Rose Lake. The purity of the Heroin could be traced if it surfaced, or had it already? Shawn was thinking about Deputy Abron's comments from the barn at Rose Lake. Someone had to have found the missing items, hidden over a century from view. He notified the FBI, requesting help in looking into the sale of the coins.

Deputy Monroe let him know, on the QT the next morning, that several had been sold to a buyer in Hong Kong within the past year. The captain called his counterpart over in Coeur d'Alene, Captain June Croop, requesting more on the investigation into the newfound drug lab at the Nelson homestead. Deputy Price was already working with Lieutenant Tony Bara, coordinating data found between the two agencies. Tony and Pat, like Abron, were thinking of the double homicides as two different unrelated entities.

*****

Spokane

"I wouldn't call this a shake-up," said Saunders. The captain was updating Donnie Webb at the DA's office. "Abron somehow managed to find the right path into an investigation. Call it luck, but I don't think so. It has happened too often in the last six months."

"Can his body take the pounding?" asked Donnie.

"We haven't seen any signs of pain or slowing down. Our best, Terry and Ron, have been ordered to watch him closely for any physical or mental problems. Both have assured me he's 110 percent. I've positioned him as our liaison to Sergeant Gwen in San Bernardino, sharing legal expertise when appropriate. Ron and Terry are coordinating with Montana law enforcement."

"Keep me posted, Captain. And keep Abron out of shooting situations." Donnie ended the call with Shawn.

Call it intuition. Call it luck. Kelsey's mind worked twenty-three hours a day on problem-solving. That same day, on the way home, a piece of the puzzle emerged from somewhere in Kelsey's thought process. It had been bothering him since he had spoken on the phone with Elliot Carlson over at Rose Lake. Abron, in his new role as detective, knocked on Elliot's door. "Abron is it," Elliot said as he opened the door, stepping out on to the front porch.

After formalities, Abron produced the photos he had of a man and woman. "Recognize either of them?"

Elliot thought no, at first, slightly shaking his head from side to side. But then he said, "You know, if they had hats and sunglasses, I could mistake them for the owners of the construction outfit—the company that gave the bid on the Snider's house. At least that's who Dan told me they were. But as far as I know, those two never came back even after getting the job."

"Do you remember what kind of a vehicle they were driving that day?" asked Abron.

"Yes, a white four-door Mercedes Benz. Looked brand-new and very expensive."

"Sure about the make?"

"Positive," replied Elliot. "Those cars aren't seen very often on these dirt roads."

Later that afternoon, Abron put in a call to Terry and Ron. With both his cohorts on the phone, he unloaded the information. "I went by Elliot's earlier this afternoon, showing him those photos of the McCoys. He's pretty sure they were at the Sniders to bid a construction job prior to the Nelson homicides. He mentioned they were wearing hats and sunglasses. Then he positively identified the color and make of the vehicle they drove to Rose Lake. A brand new white Mercedes Benz four-door sedan with a Spokane dealership license-plate holder."

"Holy shit." said Terry as Ron whistled in the phone. "The Captain know?" asked Terry.

"You're the first. Go gettum. I've got a date tonight with Izzy."

"Where to?" asked Terry.

"Remember the old Black Angus downtown, on the river? Great steaks, seafood. Izzy's favorites. Captain keeps reminding me to take it easy during this investigation, but I can't."

Terry jumped in. "You just worry about taking care of Izzy, making her happy. We all figure she's our adopted sister from the Bump Inn."

*****

*****

Recently promoted Lieutenant Terry Hollander was coordinating the effort to investigate mill superintendents and their connection to the unions that worked within. Thanks to some help from the feds, scores of possible payoff and embezzlement files were handed over to his team. The DA's office was given three names attributed to the payments. All three men were union members. Lieutenant Hollander's team, in cooperation with the DA's office, ascertained that the amounts under suspicion totaled north of a million dollars in the last twenty-four months before the feds came knocking. Terry's team had already been handed FBI/DA data confirming that $350,000 had been skimmed from the retirement fund locally.

One of the three suspects involved drew a red flag with law enforcement—Moses Chavez, a brother to the Pete Chavez that had tried to assassinate Officer Kelsey in the hospital. Adding to the red flag, his attorney of record was the now-deceased David McCoy. David had represented Moses in a court appearance for assault and battery. The battery was so severe one of the victims was hospitalized for several days. The wife had also been battered, sustaining a fractured jaw, in the same altercation—allegedly when Moses Chavez hit her with a golf club. Curiously, charges were later dropped when the victims recanted their original statements to the police, reasoning that they couldn't tell the difference between Pete and Moses even though evidence indicated two persons had committed the battery. Moses had been incarcerated the day of the incident. Bail set at $50,000 was paid within 48 hours by his attorney.

When the Idaho Sheriff's Department tried to interview the Sniders, the injured husband and wife had disappeared from the house by Rose Lake. Deputies entered the house when they decided something was suspicious. They found a mess. More like a crime scene. Somebody had ransacked the house. Every room was in disarray. Furniture, draperies, and appliances had been left behind. Curiously, the refrigerator and freezer were mostly empty, as were the closets. No forwarding address was available. There were no clues as to where they were headed. Deputy Terry Hollander was shocked when he learned the couple's identity, Cora and Dan Snider.

Cleared by Captain Saunders to visit the DA's office within the courthouse, Terry and Ron were talking to Assistant DA Cynthia Berdot outside a courtroom. Terry questioned, "How would Moses come up with the bail money so quickly? How much would it have cost Moses and maybe Pete to get the charges dropped and have the victims disappear without a trace?"

Cynthia knew the case but was caught off guard, hesitating then answering, "You already know about bail amounts. Paying off the Sniders is a pretty large leap, don't you think?" Cynthia then switched gears, handing them new information that wasn't available in any of the original reports. "Did you know that Joe and Wesley Nelson owned the Snider property? They also hold the deed to 160 acres of meadow and forest to the southeast of there. To this day, it's tied up in probate court. The official plat map lists both as Black Rock Gulch," she added.

"How long has the DA known this?" asked Terry.

"Since the Nelsons were murdered," she replied. "I'm due in court. My office is available to you any-time, by appointment." Cynthia turned, unsmiling, and headed for the courtroom.

*****

Because of his education and "Gwen type" investigative doggedness, Abron's assets were still gaining in value with Captain Saunders. "Detective, rather than forensics, through these investigations." He was speaking to Christian. "I know you have a lot on your plate, but I need Abron's help in the field. Our assets are stretched to the limit. He and Gwen were best of friends, which could help us in coordinating with San Bernardino. The men found murdered are the same persons of interest that sold the gold coins to the pawnshop. Selling them for hundreds of thousands less than they're worth is a pretty good indicator they were on the run when their luck ran out. Gwen and Kelsey will work on why. Caine, can you hold down the fort a while without Kelsey?"

Christian shot back, "Abron's good, it seems, at everything he's involved with except staying out of harm's way. Captain, we'll manage."

Later that day, Captain Saunders called Abron, confirming Deputy Kelsey's part in the investigation.

Saunders was fortunate to have two sheriff's deputies involved in forensics. With the team of civilian employees in that department headed by Caine, needed reports would be on time. Information into both cases was piling up. Now a third double-homicide case was added to the mix. Saunders felt that Kelsey and Gwen would identify the older perp, if given time. The deputies made the POI on camera, in two separate sequences, talking to the would be killers, now deceased.

The two were shot while walking from a bar to the street. *Not the work of a senior citizen*, he thought to himself. Captain Saunders needed to know where he came from as much as his identity.

*****

Spokane

That night, over dinner, both ordered strawberry margaritas, one of the more popular specialties from the restaurant's bar. It was Isabel instigating the action when she said, "We should take it easy on these. They go down fast, and you know what they say, 'Tequila makes her clothes fall off.'"

Abron shouted, "Waiter, another round of strawberry margaritas." Later that night, the deal was sealed. It was at Izzy's apartment. She and Abron didn't sleep that night, neither one wanting to see it end and both wishing the sun wouldn't rise. Isabel served bacon and cheddar omelets with toast and coffee knowing Abron was running late but hesitant to leave Izzy's company. Abron was speechless, not wanting or knowing how to say goodbye. He stood and finally started his goodbyes through the bathroom door. Isabel softly spoke, "Wait," then erotically slithered out, wearing a black fishnet bodysuit and high heels. Abron was three hours late for his meeting with the other deputies.

The list of union members possibly involved in the recent murders and cover-ups was growing as were the POIs outside the plant. The body count now totaled seven, plus two missing persons—the Sniders. Cora and Dan had not been seen in over two years. Their sons in Libby, Montana, had been increasingly concerned as months passed with no sign of their vacationing parents. Arnie and Al had been checking with the CDA Sheriff's Department on an increased basis. Six months after the disappearance, the file noted two checks were mailed to the twins. Both sons received $75,000 cashier checks, arguably sent via the mail, by their parents. The note within gave little reasoning for the gifts. The signatures and handwriting looked forged to Al and Arnie. The message itself reeked of suspicion, saying that the twin's parents were going to use the rest of the monies from the sale of the property to travel. Both Snider boys swore under questioning that the note had to be fake. Al stated that his parents never used printing to sign anything. The envelope containing the checks was postmarked out of Walla Walla, Washington. It was Arnie that reiterated, "My parents never owned the house at Rose Lake."

*****

Bitterroot National Forest; Idaho, Montana

Dillon Robinson had been practically raised with a rifle in hand, stalking the Bitterroot for game. He killed a bull elk at eleven years of age. His dad taught him how to dress out the meat and transport it for hanging. Robinson learned to track and hunt with a bow and arrow before his fifteenth birthday. From bear to bighorn sheep, he had killed and tasted them all before he was eighteen. Dillon had been taught to treat all ladies with respect. His mom was catered to by his father through his school years in Missoula. Dad would tell him, "She's my princess forever."

When Dillon began working in the woods, many opportunities presented themselves for him to make extra money guiding hunters to the elk and deer herds found in the wilds. Within two years of his first successful hunting party, the word got around. His skills had a premium value. While logging west of Missoula, Dillon's dad was injured by a deadfall incident that left him disabled. In a few short years, the bank took their home and acreage. The bottle separated Dillon's mom and dad. Dillon Robinson was mentally scarred by all that happened. He tried to solve every problem that came up in his family life. When he failed, a cancer of evil began to take hold. The world was not fair. With the exception of his dad convincing him to treat all women with respect, all bets were off. He would take what he wanted, when he needed it.

*****

Deputies Ron Rowe, Terry Hollander, Abron Kelsey, Christian Caine, Pat Price, and now Jake Monroe were the main players within the Bump Inn posse. Monroe was sticking to the plan he and Captain Saunders had developed. Not even the posse knew his secrets. Jake envied his coworkers. dreaming of someday being like them and not having to leave wife and kids for weeks on end. *Four more years, and I can take a retirement and work somewhere like Spokane with family in tow.*

The posse were seated at their table in the corner of the Bump Inn. Midway through summer, Pacific storms were now producing thunderstorms with hot humid days and cool too-cold evenings. Isabel was serving her favorite customers another round. She noticed Abron wasn't acting like his affable self. They had been living together for more than a month. To her, he seemed out of character. When Abron abruptly left the inn without saying goodbye, Izzy was visibly shaken. The deputies, mainly Pat (now Abron's partner), were under fire by Isabel. When Pat gave her the news that Abron was taking a transfer to Minnesota at the end of the month, an explosion occurred right in front of all who were in the Bump that night.

The explosion was enormous. Isabel knocked over two tables, beer glasses flying everywhere. She then started swearing at everyone around her while rushing toward the door to the parking lot. Pat would later tell Abron that "She was a category 5 hurricane aimed at your ass." As she crashed through the door to the outside, Isabel saw Abron, on his knees, with her parents behind him. The three were backlit by four squad cars flashing in the dark. Her fury was impossible to hide, but her thermometer was falling, especially when she turned and saw the entire crowd at the Bump Inn standing behind her. It was a setup. She was beside herself with anger for letting them—him—get the best of her.

"Isabel, I love you with all my heart and soul. Please marry me."

"How dare you!" she yelled as she stormed through onlookers and went back inside of the Bump. Somewhere near was the distinct sound of a barn owl. It was so quiet everyone heard it. The moment of silence was quickly broken before anyone could catch their breath. Izzy came charging back out of the inn with a bottle of tequila in her hand. "It's about time," she said. "I've never wanted anything so bad that it hurt. Until you came along. You are my dream come true. Damn it. Yes, I'll marry you forever." And the celebration began where the two bumped into each other.

*****

Spokane Sheriff's Department

"With what we know now about the dead pair in California, I can't figure how it all ties together," said Officer Price.

Abron surprised Pat with his next comment. "What if these three double murders are not related? What if they are three totally separate incidents—two linked, one solo?"

"How so?" asked Pat.

"In the beginning, before the Nelsons were killed, there was an intense feud broiling with the Sniders. That's according to Elliot Carlson. Last night I got a call from Terry. He and Ron had just interviewed the Snider twins over in Libby. They told Terry there was no bitterness between their parents and the Nelsons. In fact, for many years as neighbors, they played pinochle every Sunday, taking turns hosting dinner and cards at their farmhouses."

A flag went up in Kelsey's subconscious when Pat abruptly changed the subject. Brushing off the significance of the new information, Pat commented, "That's hard to believe." Price then followed up with questions. "Where did all the money come from if the Nelsons weren't connected to the payoffs and corruption within the factory and the union? Legal fees, construction at their farms, and the Sniders' disappearance. Aren't we back to square 1? Without illegal union money, all motives would be bogus."

"Pat, what if there is another source of wealth? Monies that would tie the San Bernardino killings to the Nelsons at the same time eliminating the McCoys from the equation. Let's say they were only in the picture for their legal expertise."

Again, Pat chimed in. "How does Bob Balicki and this Bryce McCallen, both union leaders, fit in? Or do they?" asked Pat.

Abron tried not to present a questioning look. *Another change of direction,* he thought. *But why?* "Let's jump ahead to a conversation that Izzy had with the professors researching the train robbery," said Abron, "the experts that Captains Saunders and Captain Croop enlisted to help verify that missing pot of gold. All three conclude it was possible. What if someone found it? Both professors intimated to Izzy a wild story of train robberies, shoot-outs, murder, gold nuggets, opium, laudanum, and extremely valuable gold coins. None of which was ever recovered from the late 1800s to present day. Every bit of what they told her was ferreted out of period newspaper articles, weeklies, dailies, train logs, and law enforcement reports found in areas between Spokane and Butte."

"Lost treasure?" queried Pat.

Abron continued, "A fortune waiting to be discovered. Possibly by the Nelsons! Could they have used some of that wealth to pay off the Sniders for property damages? Or was that incident a lie? Terry came away from the same interview with another Elliot falsehood. Al and Arnie verified what Cynthia Berdot told Ron Rowe: The Nelsons owned the Sniders' farm and house. Dan and Cora were renting."

Pat's expression showed no emotion. His eyes blinked with a slight twitch of his cheeks. Abron didn't miss it. He was baiting Pat. "Sounds to me like a pretty wild treasure hunt. Almost too good to be true. How much money are we talking about?" asked Pat.

"Both professors agreed the sum total could exceed three hundred million at today's gold prices."

"Have you told Saunders?" asked Price.

"He's in the loop. Cap enlisted Isabel to be his liaison to the professors."

"Why Isabel?" Price asked.

"Izzy is minoring in Northwest history. Saunders enlisted her to work as a go-between with Tony Bara's professors. Speaking of Tony, one of his officers, Maria Flores, has become good friends with Isabel. They met while participating, in one way or another, at a fundraiser for graduating high school seniors, teens in need of financial help for college. Oddly enough, the Nelsons and McCoys were among several dozen benefactors over the last four years." Kelsey didn't garner so much as a flinch from Pat when Maria's name was purposefully brought into the conversation. "The Nelsons worked at hourly paying jobs but yet were part of the governing board responsible for the raising and distribution of the funds. Isabel was the one who came up with the idea that Joe and Wesley must have found the booty from the train robbery, secreting it away. She also researched land ownerships in North Idaho for our captain, finding to be true what Cynthia told Ron."

"Who knew," replied Pat.

Abron fired back, "Hopefully only law enforcement."

"I meant, 'who knew,' as in, 'that's incredible.' It's a crazy tale," commented Pat.

"It's even crazier when you add police corruption and cover-ups," stated Abron.

Pat had an odd look while asking Abron, "Police corruption?"

"Possibly. This web is larger than anyone could have imagined. But it's showing signs of unraveling," Abron ended.

*****

Joan saw Abron walk through the door and head for his favorite booth. Abron hadn't been around for a couple of weeks. Pouring coffee, she asked Abron about that little blond he had mentioned a few weeks earlier. He smiled then thought, *Joan needs to be brought up to date with Izzy.* He started, "We had our first date. Her name is Isabel Davis. But to me, she's Izzy." Joan could see Officer Kelsey begin to light up. He was always friendly but reserved about his job and private life. When Abron was almost killed, she didn't hear about it for almost two weeks. Joan had wondered what had happened to her regular breakfast patron. She heard it from two Spokane police officers seated at the counter.

"It was one of their forensic officers. His name is Irish."

Joan asked "Abron Kelsey?"

"That's it—Abron."

Joan was all ears when told the story.

"Can anyone see him?" she asked.

The younger of the two policemen answered, "They've got him under lock-and-key security, making sure the perpetrators don't come back to finish the job."

Joan was amazed and worried. Her regulars were like her kids. The police officers gave her the information on his whereabouts. That afternoon, she sent Kelsey a get-well card, telling him breakfast was on her when he got better. She never knew about the second attack on his life until now when Joan asked about the wound on his hand while filling his coffee cup.

"Abron, you truly have the luck of the Irish on your side."

"I do now," he said, beaming as he added, "I got to call her Izzy and she said yes!"

*****

"Maria, come in," said Izzy. "Coffee, tea, ice water?"

"Iced tea. What did you find out from the professors?" Maria asked.

"Laskowski and Wood have really put in the hours since I spoke with John at that fundraiser. The first report was, I thought, very thorough. But Woody Bob, as his students call him, emailed this to me last night:

> FYI, good hunting
> CC: Saunders, Berdot, Webb, Gwen, Hollander, Bara
>
> Missing person report circa 1880s: "Owner Molly and hired man Henry of the Silver Saddle way station, on the north fork of the Coeur d'Alene River, missing. They were last seen, by another hired hand, journeying southwest in a buggy."
>
> A further report found, from one year later: "Missing pair have still not

turned up. Foul play being investigated. Silver Saddle Inn reopening services."

Also, this from a Pinkerton report, same time period: "Agents have traced the movement of valuable properties stolen in a train robbery west of Butte, Montana, to the St. Joe River in Idaho territory. Trail ran cold at this point. Investigation ongoing."

Good hunting.

Signed,
Bob

PS. Enjoyed our meeting, love to see you again.

"It's hard to believe there could be a treasure with these murders," stated Maria.

"Abron's theory may be coming to light," replied Izzy. "It's crazy, but Abron mentioned to me that the most dangerous persons may be connected to the missing fortune. Abron thinks that, possibly, the treasure is the reason for some of the killings. If there is a treasure. Environmental cover-ups at the plant could have caused other deaths. Maria, he also warned me not to tell anyone of his theory."

"I don't understand?" said Maria.

"There are a lot of pieces to this puzzle. Some of the pieces include persons not afraid to kill for the right price. He warned me not to involve anyone with his ideas. Maria, I shouldn't have told you this. Abron as much as swore me to silence. But you have the same involvement with most of the facts that I have. I think we both should be wary of possible dangers. Let's keep this between us."

"Izzy, I wouldn't betray your confidence. Will you keep me in the loop?"

There was a loud knock on the apartment door that startled Izzy and Maria. "Nobody comes calling this late in the evening, and Abron's not here," Isabel whispered.

"Oh, come on, Izzy," said Maria, "you're taking this too seriously. I'll answer the door."

"It's my door. It could be my parents. You sit here and enjoy your tea."

Maria's mind was in second gear. She began to take her part in this more seriously. Maria was stoutly built yet ladylike—attractive, quiet, and always asking but not telling.

She was raised in Boise but landed at the police academy after trying college at the U of I, Moscow. A couple of inches taller than Isabel, she stood and then sat with shoulders back perfect posture. Curiously, her thoughts weren't of the knock at the door. She was, subconsciously, dreaming of fellow Officer Pat Price and the sex they had had the night before. Maria would protect him first under any circumstances.

"Pat, enter. What a surprise," Isabel greeted. "Maria Flores is here also. She's one of your fellow sheriff's deputies out of CDA."

"I saw her car out front," stated Pat. "This is just a quick stop." Barely acknowledging Maria, he continued with "Abron was worried because you weren't answering your phone?"

Isabel was embarrassed enough to tell a white lie. "Woops, forgot to turn it back on. I turned it off at eight this morning. Apparently, my résumé was given to a headhunting organization by one of my councilors. I guess my field of study is in demand."

"Who would have thought?" Pat stole a glance at Maria. His thoughts immediately turned carnal.

"Where is Abron? asked Izzy. "You and he are always together since partnering."

"Your future husband is neck-deep in these homicides. Saunders has now made him the liaison between the FBI and law enforcement within our three-state area. He wanted me to let you know he's on an emergency flight to Chicago. Also, to remind you to turn on your cell. So message delivered. Are you all right?"

"Of course." Then it hit home. "Chicago," said Isabel. A mild look of fright came over her. "When will he come back?"

"Answer your phone. He said he's tried to call you for hours. I'm on the run, duty calls." Isabel thanked Pat, catching him nodding a smile to Maria as he was leaving.

"That was fast. He normally likes to chat for a while. Maybe it's because he's covering for Abron?" she told Maria.

After Deputy Price departed, Isabel asked, "I didn't know you knew Pat."

"Just in passing" was Maria's answer. "That's the first I've seen of Pat Price in weeks. I don't think we've ever even been properly introduced."

Isabel queried, "How would he know that your car was out front?" Then, quickly, Izzy apologized before Maria could act. "Sorry, I'm beginning to think that some of Abron's suspicious ways are creeping into my psyche, freaking me out."

"Well, after what you went through with Abron and his two near-death episodes, I wouldn't count out that a little paranoia was attached to whatever seeped in," commented Maria. "Maybe," she added, "he saw my car parked near Abron's. Those two hooked up for work in the parking lot a few times after your beau got out of class. I will say, Pat is a hunk." At that moment, Isabel tried not to tip her hand. Several question marks had spooked her. Later, after Maria had headed home, Isabel wrote down a couple of those questioning ideas to ask Abron about. "Coincidence," she wrote. "Maria and Pat, inside our apartment, sharing those looks between them while pretending no to know one another." Isabel hoped her Abron knew something about the two—her final thought was, why hadn't Abron mentioned Pat meeting him at Gonzaga?

Isabel and Maria had become close after Isabel's accidental foray into the detective business. It seemed to her that Maria was enthusiastic to learn Abron's and her thoughts on the investigations. Their get-togethers seemed to be happening more often, the bulk of which were instigated by Maria. Other questions began to take shape. "Why is she so insistent on union involvement? Doesn't she understand the depth of a multimillion treasure?" It was another question for Abron along with the thought *Maybe I shouldn't have given her everything from the Laskowski/Wood report.* Isabel had no way of knowing that Maria had headed straight from Izzy's condo to Pat's condo.

Moments after Maria departed, Izzy's phone rang. "Abron," she opened.

He immediately began before she could say another word. "Isabel, I've been worried about you. Is everything okay?"

"All is well. I just forgot to charge my phone. Then I butt-called my parents sometime this afternoon, rendering it dead. You sound so serious. Are you okay?"

"Izzy, go to your parents' house and spend tonight and tomorrow. I'll explain when I get home in two days. Call in sick to everything you have planned on Friday. Saturday, I'll come straight from the airport to the Davenport Hotel. I'm meeting Christian and Captain Saunders there at nine p.m. We'll talk when the bar closes. I'm on to something. The FBI is helping our case, but I must stay here through tomorrow for a clearer picture of the players."

"Come on, Abron, don't be so cloak-and-dagger," Isabel replied.

"Izzy, I love you dearly and would never attempt to boss you around except when lives could be in danger. Please, this once, do what I ask."

She agreed and said, "I'll leave now. Do I need to call Pat or the captain?"

Abron then said something she wouldn't forget, words that enhanced her suspicions from earlier that evening. "Talk to no one, just leave ASAP. Isabel, there's a rat in our department, and there may be a nest of them. I'll explain when I get back. Don't let on to anyone where you're located. Slip in the back door at the Davenport, after nine, Saturday."

*****

"They never should have attacked Officer Kelsey, and we should never have trusted those nitwit brothers. The Sniders were another mistake," she said. "If they were still alive, I think Dan and Cora would have gladly taken a cash offer and moved to Canada. Our brilliant strategist that started this seems to be leading us all to jail or worse. Poor decisions are now acting as a catalyst for the Spokane Sheriff's Office. The Rose Lake investigation is back in full swing. The misdirection toward the union is starting to fail. We've all been paid a lot of money. Until now, none of us has had to do much but turn a blind eye." Silence on the phone. "Officer Kelsey attacked in the hospital. Are you kidding me? Now Pete's death leads them to his brother, Moses. Do we know if he's dependable?" she asked Tony. "John and I have already decided that he must go. It's in your hands. You were the one who said Pete was willing and capable. We never thought Moses would be in the picture. They were, at one time, both union."

"Hold it. Back up. I recommended Pete for his ability to keep his mouth shut and take care of some of our dirty work. I never intended to use him as a hit man in broad daylight!" said Tony.

The lady that seemed to be in charge of the conversation brought up a second problem that also had to be dealt with. "You, Pat, and Maria need to keep them focused on the money siphoned from the aluminum plant. The perception that those monies equate to lives should be your focus. We have an idea that should nudge it to the forefront. Our explosives expert is going to rattle some fences."

A third party nervously spoke into the speakerphone, "Isabel and Abron could be on to us. I went to Isabel's apartment for an update on the coin search. Unknowingly, Pat showed up to give her information on Kelsey and his doings in Chicago. Isabel's phone was off all day. Abron phoned her several times then sent Pat to check. I got the feeling something was up."

Then Pat added, "None of us have been seen together before that time. To show up, even by accident, could trigger suspicion from them."

The lady in charge spoke again, "A major concern, Pat?"

"Not at this time and maybe never," he answered.

She then stated, "With the Sniders at the bottom of Lake Pend Oreille, our main concern, not yours, is the Nelson property and investigation. Isabel and Abron may have to be dealt with. Isabel is digging into ownerships of the lands surrounding Rose, Killarney, and

Newman Lakes. Knowing that changes things on our end. Both of you need to back off from any conversations or meetings with those two, if possible. John and I will talk and plan our next move." Speaking to Tony, she said, "Has everyone's payments arrived on time offshore?" All three said yes with smiles.

*****

Eight years prior to the father and son homicides, Joe purchased the eighty acres he and his wife and son were to call home. Joe's wife had been diagnosed with a type of cancer that would lead to her death in months. Her wish, to her husband, was to live away from the city lights, raising their son in a country environment. Joe worshipped her and would, no matter what, figure a way to bring her wishes home. Joe Nelson had a great-uncle that, for years, had told the story about the family homestead where he and his siblings were raised. It was located in Northern Idaho, to the east of the Rose and Killarney Lakes and up a wooded canyon called Black Rock. The story stuck in his mind the first time he heard it at eleven years of age. Joe was dissuaded from putting too much truth into what his uncle was telling him as his uncle Clyde was a notorious family drunk. But Joe, as a kid, had heard the stories so often over the next several years he could imagine himself exploring the meadow and pine-covered hills. The meadow containing a rock-lined hand-dug well. The well that so many of his great-uncle's stories were centered around.

But time slipped away. After high school then trade school, marriage, job, and a child, his uncle Clyde's stories along with the pictures in his mind had all but faded away. Facing his wife's condition, those visions and thoughts began to once again take shape. When the decision to move was made, he found the Rose Lake acreage located across from the old homestead to the west. In less than a month, the property closed. Already packed in anticipation, the family was soon on their way to North Idaho, taking Stella and Wesley away from the heat, traffic congestion, and seasonal tule fog of Fresno, California.

Joe and family spent the first four weeks getting settled. It was mid-May and time for a garden. This was his first attempt at vegetable gardening. His wife was too weak to put many hours into the project. Joe, with Wesley by his side, tilled up almost a quarter acre next to the house and barn. Joe planted what would end up to be over three-hundred pounds of potatoes from russets to German fingerlings, purple potatoes, and goldens. He later discovered they had been a little overzealous with most of the crop. His corn eventually yielded two hundred ears, and broccoli plants were still being harvested after the first snow fell in mid-October.

Stella began to noticeably fade around the Fourth of July in their second year. Before the first snow, she was bedridden. The move to North Idaho proved to be right. Stella's attitude toward life turned back to positive, possibly affording her many extra months of happiness with her family. The move was also good for Joe and Wesley. The years in Fresno were hard on Joe Nelson. He hated his job in the city working for a package delivery service through heat, traffic, and never-ending deliveries. Ten years on the job began to feel like a lifetime. Now two years later, living in Idaho with his wife dying and the job of keeping the household going, young son in tow, and mounting bills, Joe's anxiety and desperation resurfaced.

Two weeks after the funeral, Joe took his son for a ride across the highway into Black Rock Gulch. While driving, he told his son the story that Great-Uncle Clyde had ingrained in him so long ago. Uncle Clyde would tell Joe what Joe was telling his son now. Only Joe told it as best he could remember without embellishment. "My parents and your great-uncle and aunt owned lots of property near here. This side of the highway, where we live, once belonged to Clyde's family. Further down the highway, on the east side going toward St. Maries, there are 120 acres that we own thanks to your grandparents and your uncle. Rest their souls.

"The acreage was originally willed to your uncle Bob when I expressed no interest in it. But Bob didn't want it. He hated snow, insects, unspoiled land, and seasonal changes. Wesley, you weren't old enough to remember your uncle Bob, but I'm pretty sure he wouldn't have liked you. Because he hated your mom and me. Someday, when we have time, I'll tell you why. Uncle Bob did one thing right by us. When Stella was dying, he quitclaim deeded the 120 acres to us. To him, I'm sure he thought it was bestowing a burden on our family and was happy to do it. He had no kids or wife, and his lifetime partner died a few months before Bob. I'm telling you this because the land will all be yours eventually.

"The original Nelson homestead has a stream running along the southern edge. The pasture was surrounded by pine-filled hills. When I was a boy, Dad used to tell me about an old falling-apart boiler made of rocks, sand, and mud. The boiler used to create steam to run a small sawmill located up the draw to the east of where I'm taking you. That sawmill produced the lumber that helped build your great-grandparents' home after they immigrated from Haugesund, Norway. I remember a couple of ramshackle cabins a short distance from the boiler. Dad used to tell me about fishing a gold coin out of a man-made well located on the southern side of the meadow. The well went dry only once that he could remember. I always wanted to climb into the well and search for more coins or maybe an old whisky bottle that Clyde said were on the bottom, just below the surface.

"I'm guessing that jobs were hard to find for your grandpa and uncle back then. I'm pretty sure that reason forced a move to St. Regis, Montana, for work at the local sawmill. Your grandpa referred to the work as 'pulling green chain.' Dad and I always wondered where that coin came from originally. We kind of agreed that a mill worker or woodsman somehow dropped it down the well where it sat for decades until Dad found it. We were going to go back someday but never had the chance.

"Son," said Joe, "today's the day. With our dry summer and this rope ladder, I'm going to climb down there."

They both had about given up their search for the well. The south rim of the meadow was about a half-mile long and covered with trees and thick underbrush. Joe and Wesley were reaching frustration fast when Wesley asked, "Could the well be outside of the pines but inside those birch trees? I think they're new to the meadow. They almost look out of place. Don't they, Dad?"

Joe replied, "Birch trees need water and lots of it. Wesley, you may have found the well." The brush was tall and plentiful, so they headed straight into the middle of the stand. Joe spotted it first. It looked like a crumbling pile of rocks from where they stood. The brush and birch trees made it difficult to find until they were twenty feet away. "Try not to disturb anything. We'll keep this location to ourselves." Joe was able to clear part of the well brush so they could drop their ladder. "We'll need to carry out any knocked-down brush and burn it somewhere else. We also need to take a different line out to the meadow and not leave prints. Just in case we find something."

After all these many years of Joe and his relatives before him banging up that dirt road to his grandparents' homestead. he thought, *The bumps and ruts are still about the same.* The road had survived washouts and heavy lumber truck use over the years. It was still passable today with a high-clearance vehicle. Joe and Wesley could tell that the road had seen little travel since the snow melted and they had come calling. Likewise, nobody had found the well. Now, down in the well, the last step was a doozy for Joe, who shouted, "The water is waist-deep and cold. We're going to need a sump pump along with our generator to make it possible to see the bottom." Joe climbed out with much effort due to the extra pounds in water weight.

"What good will pumping the water out do? Won't it just fill back up?" asked Wesley.

"Look at my clothes, son. Everything down there is stagnant. I think the water is standing from rain and snowfall. I couldn't find a source of fresh water seeping into the bottom. But it's so dark and murky nothing can be found until that slop is siphoned out.

*****

Bob Balicki was relaxing on his veranda overlooking Flathead Lake to his southeast. The FBI's probe had come to nothing. He believed himself to be in the clear, untouchable. Bob was a product of the mob-run unions out of Chicago. He began an association with the underworld just a year after graduating from high school. His uncle introduced him to a small group of street toughs that were paid well for occasional jobs. Over the next year, he earned a reputation of being the toughest kid on the block. Bob would take care of whatever he was asked to do. For this, the bosses he worked for enlisted him in the local trucking union. They placed him in the office instead of driving. Within a few short months, he was involved with graft, cover-ups, and many other wrongdoings.

The point of no return came three years into his employment—murder, his first of a few. The target was a union member that had started to brag about his local's business. Bob handled it alone, explaining to his boss, "I want no witnesses and nobody around to fuck it up. Tell me where and when." The police never found a body or a witness. The hit was so clean Balicki gained a new level of interest from his handlers.

Bob Balicki and Bryce McCallen were on the same page. Both had covered their trails well over the years. They had gained the respect of higher-ups. Bob's home and his extravagant lifestyle were easily painted over through a false inheritance and offshore accounts. He and Bryce were from the "old school" in Illinois—the school of hard knocks where they first met. Both men were starting to feel that old itch of violence creeping in. Matters had to be attended to if the stream of money was going to continue to flow out of the Northwest.

Bob punched the number for Bryce as he sat in solitude. The call was short and neutral. Both were careful not to give away the purpose of the conversation. It seemed to the FBI and Montana law enforcement that the reason for the call was just to touch bases and set up a meeting somewhere between Missoula and Spokane. The FBI would track both persons. Bryce, who had recently moved to Libby, Montana, and Balicki from Whitefish. The payout of sixty million to the EPA by the aluminum plant and its subsidiaries would slow the flow of currency into Chicago. The bosses were not happy. The cleanup of the dumping and water pollution would take at least five years, as would the payments to the government agency overseeing the problem. Only union dues plus small amounts from the local retirement fund could be expected to line mob pockets.

Bob and Bryce were needed to plug leaks, if they occurred, before and after the hearings. All arrested were union members except for three plant company men. Several arrested could be put next to former union bosses in place before Balicki and McCallen arrived. Some could possibly spotlight Illinois. The main players in Spokane were bailed by the union. The rest were left to Bob and Bryce to clean up.

*****

Maria Flores and Pat Price were in bed at her house when the doorbell rang. They both knew that to be discovered together, by anyone, had the potential of ruining their future, even costing them their lives. All four conspirators had been warned to stay as far away from each other as possible. At all times. They each had received substantial amounts of money, with more to come. Maria and Pat knew there was no turning back. The monies gained would allow them a new future somewhere far away. Maria went to the door while Pat, gun at the ready, hid in the bedroom. The surprised look on her face couldn't be missed. "Abron, you're supposed to be in Chicago."

"Just got in. Your place was on the way home, so I thought I'd drop in."

"I would invite you in, but I'm not dressed and what would your Isabel say?"

"Actually, Izzy is why I'm here. We finally connected over the phone thanks to my partner, Pat Price. I was back east when she mentioned that you didn't seem yourself the last time you two met. Are you okay?

And if not, is there anything Isabel or I could do to help?"

"Thank you, Abron. Tell Isabel that all is okay. I had an urgent call from my brother over in Portland before I saw Izzy. He needed money ASAP, and my mind was wandering, trying to come up with a way to get it to him the next morning. So my conversation sense was sadly lacking. I hope I didn't say anything to Isabel that was too far out?"

"I'll report to her when I get home. I'm glad all is okay." Goodbyes over, Abron departed.

Maria wondered out loud when Pat was beside her, "Something is going on. Deputy Kelsey has never visited my door, and why did he mention your name?"

"Paranoia?" Pat asked.

"Abron Kelsey looked right through me," she responded. That's when their adrenaline level hit a new high. Both saw the pair of half-filled wineglasses sitting in plain sight on the table.

Later that same evening, after he had departed from Maria's, Christian and Abron were conversing in the bar at the Davenport Hotel. It was a meeting spot shared. Isabel's employment and the privacy of the booths in the lounge made it ideal for their work. Abron had set up their meeting while waiting for his flight home from Chicago, asking Christian to make sure Saunders was present. When Saunders joined them, pleasantries were exchanged and drinks ordered. Kelsey started in. "Until now, our team had thought everything Elliot told us was the truth. Terry's and Ron's interview with the Snider twins threw his credibility out the window. How much could Elliot be involved with? Why was he lying?"

Caine shook his head. "I never once doubted the man. He's trying to cover something up, misleading the investigation."

"Would a search warrant help?" asked Captain Saunders.

"We need it ASAP," answered Kelsey.

"I'll enlist Dot, in records, to look into his background and personal life," Shawn promised.

Abron addressed Shawn. "Christian can get more out of his house forensically than most. But if he sees us coming, we'll lose our edge."

"Only the four of us will be privy," reminded Captain Saunders. Shawn momentarily changed directions. "Not only is the relationship between the Sniders and Nelsons in question but what about the McCoys he reported seeing at the Sniders?"

"All bogus," commented Christian.

"Is there more from Chicago?" Saunders asked Abron.

"It's hard to decide where to start. I have my report coupled with theirs to give you. But I'd like to walk you through an overview before you take the time to read it." Shawn nodded for Abron to begin. "The FBI have a heated interest in the Chicago area. The phone taps they've installed are mind-boggling. If placed in our area, the taps would cover every home and business in Spokane. That's before you add live in-room listening, video feeds, and other state-of-the-art eavesdropping devices. The information given to us includes conversations about our own union local within the foundry.

"Their info seems to point to a deadly fallout with the McCoys. Phyllis was the prosecuting attorney with the DA's office. Her husband, David, shared the same bed. David had legal dealings with several union and foundry employees. Inside information! I have a CD of some phone calls between Spokane and Chicago. The union bosses are trying to steer the spotlight away from the EPA scam, retirement fund skimming, and possibly the McCoys' slaying.

"At the same time, there are several people involved with the Rose Lake and San Bernardino double homicides trying to aim the spotlight squarely on the factory problems and, again, possibly, the McCoys. Captain, there are also several lines in my report about the two attacks on my life. The information indicates local union members weren't in on it."

"That seems almost impossible, with what we know," Shawn questioned then asked, "The McCoys—how do they fit in?"

"That's where Christian's and my theory begins to evolve. We know the time line of the first two double homicides. We think the McCoys could have been a vendetta the whole time, with David in the wrong place at the wrong time. Or he was guilty of spilling union information to his wife. Phyllis was the main target all along for her part in the prosecution of the factory and unions. When she successfully shut down the flow of money to Chicago, she was executed using the Rose Lake modus operandi as cover-up. The Bureau addressed the McCoys in their findings.

"Basically, David is hardly mentioned. Phyllis has an entire chapter devoted to her. The Bureau couldn't produce any hint of a hit being placed on either of the McCoys. But all their information, when you read between the lines, points to that scenario. A mob execution! The FBI concluded—as you'll find, Captain—the money involved streaming into Chicago was large enough to warrant murder."

Both men listening to the details from Abron were mystified. Then Kelsey dropped a bomb, not knowing for sure that he wasn't signing his own death sentence. A few years earlier, Kelsey, with the USMC, had put his trust in the soldiers he was teamed with in battle operations. In the short time with the sheriff's office, he recognized Saunders and Caine as persons he would go into a firefight with.

Abron began, "Here's where their intel, concerning us, gets juicy. They have dirt, and lots of it, on several people within our own law enforcement circle. Captain Saunders, you need to read the rest by yourself. Our departments dirt, with names, starts on page 42."

After Christian and the captain departed, Kelsey phoned Isabel. "The coast is clear."

Within minutes, she appeared from behind the bar. Her look was one of confusion yet joy.

"Izzy, how's your ankle?" was the opener.

"My ankle is fine. But I can see by your hand and posture that all things physical are not right with you."

"I'll be fine." Abron smiled. *God, I love my future wife,* he thought. Then he said out loud, "Nothing is ever going to happen to you. I won't let it."

Isabel Davis was stunned. This was more serious than she had anticipated. "What's going on, Abron? Your call and now that statement have me scared spitless. I can't be in any real danger, can I?"

"Izzy, your feelings are spot-on about Maria and Pat. On the way here, from the airport, I stopped by Maria's apartment to see her reaction when I ambushed her at the door. The look was all telling. Maria has a hidden agenda outside the CDA Sheriff's. I noticed on the table behind her two unfinished glasses of wine. She said she was alone. When I got back to the car, I drove around the neighborhood and found Pat's civilian car parked a couple of blocks away instead of at his own condo. The FBI turned up offshore accounts for Maria, Pat, Tony, and Cynthia."

"Cynthia?"

"As in Spokane assistant DA Cynthia Berdot." Nodding assent, he furthered, "All four accounts were out of the same bank in the Cayman Islands. Apparently, all three of the islands are under British control, allowing information sharing with the US. I was given data from all four accounts to help in our unsolved triple double homicides. Three accounts had $800,000, but Cynthia's was at 1.2 million. There have been four deposits in each over the last three years. Feds traced the deposit trail back to a shell company in Boise. That company is the same one that recently sold some old and very valuable gold pieces to a concern out of Hong Kong."

"Are those gold coins from the Butte train robbery? And do you think the Nelson murders and the Sniders' disappearance are part of this?" Isabel asked.

"You're connecting all the right dots with just a few of the puzzle pieces. You're spot-on in both cases. Add two murders down in California to that equation. That's why the cloak-and-dagger stuff. Like it or not, you're too close to what's going on. I've got a meeting with Captain Saunders and District Attorney Donnie Webb tomorrow at first light. We are going to distance you from everything in this nightmare. Izzy, will you please move in with me full-time?"

She found humor by saying, "What a way to entice a woman into your bed." A very abrupt "No" was her reply.

Abron had heard that same reply once before. But again, Abron was stunned, totally caught off guard. Then Izzy uttered, "Not until we're married." She stayed with her parents that night and the next. The morning after the second night, she, her parents, and Abron were on a plane to Las Vegas.

*****

This time around, Joe and Wesley Nelson were prepared. Their equipment included a twenty-four-foot aluminum ladder, an electric hoist, boring equipment that could be used vertically or horizontally, shovels, buckets, electric lights, lit helmets, sump pumps, and even rubber waders. The generator would be the loudest item and would be used most frequently. Joe bought the quietest on the market. It was made quieter yet when they added custom sound-damping covers manufactured out of ten-inch thick aluminum-lined Styrofoam. Using every precaution, the father-and-son team parked a mile and a half away, hauling everything in with a small four-wheel utility vehicle pulling a five-by-six lowboy. If there was something in the well, it would be theirs.

The Nelsons started into the meadow area at sunrise and took a track least visible from the old dirt road. It took them five hours to track in, set up, and camouflage the equipment. With sump pumps on, Joe climbed down into the well and started boring vertical holes through the mud floor. He had guessed right;

the well was muddy, but very little seepage was visible. He began to fill a fifteen-gallon bucket with mud. The weight when filled was heavy but easily pulled to the top with the electric winch that Wesley was handling from above. After what Joe thought was more than a day's work down in the hole, the north side of the well began to crumble. He jumped onto the third rung of the ladder and scurried out of the hole. Joe was exhausted. They ate dinner as the sun was fading and slept to the sounds of wind in the trees and wildlife.

The next morning found Joe climbing back into the well just as daylight began to filter in over the hilltops. "Wesley, there's something down here," Joe yelled with excitement. A dozen large rocks made up most of the crumbling that Joe thought might trap him the evening before. The rocks had been put in place long ago and mortared with a dark-colored cement-type substance. "There's a hole down here on the north side of the well wall. Climb down and take a look." Joe and Wesley crowbarred more of the rock covering from the side before excitedly shining a light into what appeared to be a four-feet-by-four-feet tunnel moving away from the well shaft. With little room to maneuver, they decided to spend some time cleaning out the bottom of the well before searching the tunnel.

After lunch, Wesley, the smaller of the two, started into the tunnel, headlamp on. Both of the Nelsons were nervous. Not so much about what they would find but nervous about a cave-in that could kill. As Wesley was crawling into the tunnel, he noticed a slight upward cant from the level the bottom of the well was on. What water there was ran backward past him toward his dad. After fifteen feet of nervous crawling, Wesley found some old cedar four-by-four posts held together with rotted leather and hemp ropes. He pushed against the crumbling wood barrier that gave way instantly. The tunnel opened just slightly into a space about six feet by fourteen feet, maybe six feet high. The storage-type room was well-built, supported by eight-by-eight-inch posts. The cedar lagging above was still intact.

Wesley now had an area large enough to make a 180 and crawl headfirst back to the well. Before starting out, he spied crate-type boxes stacked on top of a rock floor in the back half of the opening. Before he could get a closer look, he panicked. Wesley scurried out of the tunnel in seconds.

"What's wrong, Wesley?"

"Dad, I can't. I won't go back in there again," he said.

"Is it dangerous, son?"

"No. I just found out I'm afraid of small enclosed places."

Joe grinned. "You're claustrophobic, that's all. Don't worry about it. I'll take it from here. Sounded like you hit something back there. Is it worth me going in to take a look?"

Excitedly, Wesley told Joe of the small open area, the cedar posts, and the stacked wooden crates. By the time Wesley finished, Joe was beside himself. Even though Joe's dad lost and never found that old twenty-dollar gold piece, Joe Nelson's mind started running wild with thoughts of treasure. The work was strenuous and tedious. Joe and Wesley had removed and hauled to the surface several of the more-than-two-dozen crates. The rough-cut cedar containers were in amazingly good condition held together with square nails that Joe had never seen before. Night had already started to enclose them at their campsite in the trees.

Anxiously, they began the process of opening the first crate. The noise, coupled with the lack of specific tools to tackle the crate, made Joe grumble to Wesley, "We can't open these here. Let's grab them all and take them back to our barn. There we can open them at our leisure."

Suddenly, there came a sound from down the meadow to the west. The small camp light was turned off as the two sat in silence. Both were nervous. They had no idea of what was in the crates, but their minds were running at high rpm. The sound grew louder, coming their way around a bank of pines on the old dirt road. No headlights were showing, but voices began to reach the Nelsons.

Joe said to his son, "Get your .270 and meet me behind the windfall."

"Why no headlights, Dad?"

Joe whispered back, "They're hunting for grouse or deer on the road, riding the fenders."

Suddenly a bright spotlight shone in their direction. Joe's and Wesley's pulse quickened. In a flash, the twelve gauge went off, an explosion thundering across the meadow amplified by the surrounding hills. The Nelsons saw two flashlights come on as two teens jumped off the fenders and headed for the dead brown grouse lying on the dirt road. The intruders on the meadow were just hunting.

"They may come back this way or head over the north ridge and down into Pinehurst. Let's hunker down and load the rest of the crates tomorrow morning. Whatever is in them, someone went to a lot of trouble making them disappear." The hunters were three teens drinking and illegally night hunting for anything they could shoot. Fortunately for both parties, the hunters never reappeared. The Nelsons slept with one eye open that night.

*****

Balicki and McCallen thought they had escaped the eyes of the law meeting at a café in Thompson Falls, Montana. Thompson Falls lay northwest, off I-90 out of St. Regis. The Clark Fork River ran west away from the continental divide along the road to their meeting. The café was always loud with customers. The people enjoying breakfast looked neutral. They were, by appearance, regulars. Balicki showed McCallen a list of several people. The list was divided into two parts—one with Bryce's name, the other Bob's. There was one word at the top: "Disappear."

After breakfast and talk of old times in Chicago, Bryce asked Bob, "Am I crazy, or is that river running uphill the wrong way?"

Balicki replied, "Not crazy, the Clark Fork runs ass backward." Bryce was the first to depart. Bob was watching the parking lot as McCallen drove off. *Clean*, he thought, taking his leave. Both men knew what to do. They had the resources to fix the mess. It would take time and planning, but it was doable in their minds. The lists were broken down into two parts: priority and essential. Priority first. Bob and Bryce were also told to be detectives by their higher-ups. Someone or a group in their area was trying to push the case against the union and illegal dumping to the forefront of law enforcement. The first stages of environmental cleanup had just started. The money train had stopped flowing east. FBI and EPA were everywhere and into almost everything connected to the plant. Erasing the names on the lists was not going to be easy.

In total, Bryce's and Bob's responsibilities were only a handful of people: union and mill persons, each with a piece of the puzzle that could lead to Chicago. Their immediate concern was to find out where, and by who, the finger-pointing bad press was coming from. Establishing a list of reporter's names and the people they interviewed began.

*****

Six years before Joe and Wesley were murdered, the pair worked long and hard transforming their barn. All three of the windows were covered on the inside. One faced north, another south, and the final west. Joe and Wesley agreed. The forty-by-forty-foot garage/barn couldn't be visually penetrated by outside eyes. Joe had the steel building erected over an existing root cellar. After the building was completed, they brought in a Bobcat front-end loader. It was a tough job getting down into the underground room. The men used a wooden ramp that was removable. They expanded the perimeter while digging the cavity deeper. Cinder-block walls were added to a concrete floor. They anchored a steel plate to the concrete area of the building's ground-level floor. They added several hinges that had to be welded on to the cover. The plate covering their underground root cellar was camouflaged with tarp and dirt. They had seen some of the wealth but never imagined the full scope of the riches. The Nelsons now had a hidden storage area that would allow time away from prying eyes.

With images of the one gold coin his father had found, Joe and Wesley began to uncrate. The first four crates contained over two-hundred pounds of a flour-like powder packaged in deteriorating bundles. Joe was certain that it was worthless stored flour. The next three crates contained small bottles labeled "Laudanum." Wesley asked what it was. "Painkillers. I think it was made from opium poppies."

"Dad," said Wesley, "let's put in an underground passage to the house. We can enter and leave from the house without being seen."

"It's worth the effort," Joe replied. The heaviest crates were at the bottom of the cache. When Joe opened the first crate, he started to holler, "Yes, yes! Son, we hit pay dirt!" Wesley couldn't understand. The crate was lined with a gunnysack material filled with brown and dark-grey looking small pebbles. Wesley knew the crate was extremely heavy for the its size. "Those are small gold nuggets, son. They've been waiting a long time for us to discover them. There must be two- or three-hundred pounds in these three boxes. This gold is worth over $1,000 an ounce."

The next two crates were lined in cedar and linen. Each box looked like a pirate treasure chest full of gold coins. "The gold coins have to be worth more than twenty dollars each. This is a fortune found. I don't know the value of it all, but it's got to be in the hundreds of thousands. When we get the chain fall in, opening and closing our steel door should be a piece of cake. How we're going to dispose of this stuff for cash must be done carefully. Some of my coworkers, even neighbors and friends, would kill for these riches."

The months of work were hard on the two. Joe had to work five days a week at the nearby aluminum plant over the state line. He helped get Wesley into the labor union and obtain a job driving trucks for the plant. "We need a truck to haul the dirt away unnoticed. Six months from now you can quit and work for us full-time, figuring a way to turn this stuff into cash."

The Spokane sheriff's team assigned to the McCoy homicides was charging forward. A meeting was called the week after Abron and Isabel tied the knot. Captain Saunders and his handpicked crew were gathered. Shawn recapped evidence to date, adding information from the two other double homicides that might or might not be related.

Terry Hollander was the first to offer input. "With all this information available, I can't get past the attack on Abron then the assassination attempt at the hospital. What did the perps hope to gain? The drug lab under the Nelsons' barn didn't amount to much. The FBI made it clear, through the found computer, that it was a small-time operation with no ties to any cartels or Chicago. The captured computer's list of contacts and clients goes nowhere."

Cap interrupted and asked Deputy Kelsey his thoughts.

"The drug lab was a cover-up to hide something larger. Heroin we found was 99.9 percent pure. That grade isn't available from the underground market in the Northwest. The Nelsons' lab wasn't producing any new product for sale. We're missing something."

Pat joined in. "Maybe the deceased that attacked you had taken over the underground lab after the deaths of Joe and Wesley. Equipment found at the lab site was new, according to Christian. So new I think it was just getting started. The updated equipment points to methamphetamine manufacturing, a more valuable product. I think we caught them early."

Captain Shawn Saunders was a patient man by nature. Patient to a point. "What the hell are you doing to me?" he asked. All noise stopped. "McCoys, not Nelsons."

Terry Hollander jumped in, segueing the team in the right direction. "Remember the piece of skin found at the McCoys that drew a match? Bryce McCallen. He's a known union higher-up that our federal friends identify with Robert Balicki. When was he in the McCoys' house and why? The condition of the skin pointed out that it was much older than when the homicides took place. I don't think Bryce was involved with those killings. He might have had other dealings with the McCoys', possibly payoffs."

Detective Ron Rowe chimed in, "Abron's theory from several weeks ago may be closest. The union was involved with the McCoys' deaths. The Nelsons and deceased POIs in San Bernardino were killed for an entirely different reason—rare coins and the drug lab. Chief, didn't Isabel, Gwen, and the professors uncover over three hundred missing gold pieces, the value in the millions?"

The newest face in Spokane law enforcement, Lieutenant Jake Monroe, spoke for the first time in front of Shawn's crew. "If all that is true, my first observations as a newbie among you points to at least two different sides that will kill to keep the monies flowing and/or hidden from view."

The meeting was interrupted by a call to Captain Saunders. "What?"—a pause—"Where?" He put down the phone and said, "A large explosion has been reported at the aluminum mill. Death and injuries. Terry, Ron, Pat, get on it. Abron, you, Christian, and Jake stay seated."

Pat hesitated, started to speak, and then turned and left with Ron and Terry. All four remaining noticed the pause.

Still seated, only one of the four was puzzled. Shawn began the explanation. "Christian, I wanted you present to get to know Jake a little better. It's important that you do. But most of what I'm about to tell you is privy to just the four of us in this room."

Shawn then handed the ball to Jake. "I'm a special investigator working with internal affairs, on loan from the FBI. Captain Saunders sent a request through District Attorney Donnie Webb to my superiors requesting help. Both of you have been cleared through my office and by Captain Saunders. No one—and I mean nobody at the Spokane Sheriff's Office or, with the exception of Webb, the DA's office—has knowledge of my intentions here."

Over the last six years, Jake Monroe had spearheaded some of the toughest internal investigations that law enforcement had to offer. He was, however, virtually unknown in the Northwest. Agent Monroe's previous investigations took place along the Atlantic corridor. Exceptional people skills coupled with an FBI education focusing on internal affairs allowed him to befriend everyone he touched. Monroe presented a facade of being a jokester, single, easy to get along with, and faithful to those he worked with. In reality, Jake's family consisted of a wife and two adolescent children. His family was located in Naples, Florida. They were used to his extended absences. The Bureau gave him carte blanche with the airlines to fly home once a month or in case of emergency. His family was never allowed to know where he was at any time for their safety and his.

Abron had "accidentally" met Monroe while in Chicago. Kelsey knew how slick Jake was. In two separate encounters, Jake had carefully pried personal information about Abron's life while not giving the younger deputy much to go on about Monroe's background. Abron was on to him at the get-go, too many questions. Jake sensed it but kept moving forward. His report to superiors had a lot to do with Abron being given clearance into his internal affairs' investigation. Jake needed someone already on the inside. Someone he could trust and depend on.

Now Christian was being indoctrinated into the small circle of professionals. Jake was beginning to see two different sides to the internal problems. The original attack on Abron and the second hospital melee was born out of need by someone positioned outside the law. That someone needed cooperation from inside Shawn's office and possibly farther reaching—into the community. In these matters, Jake was boss.

Agent Monroe needed time and their cooperation for the second part of the equation facing the department. He needed a bigger picture and clues to find out who was behind the turning of law enforcement personnel.

Jake Monroe began to school Christian, pulling no punches. "As you now know, your department and the DA's office have a few enemies working against the principles of your law enforcement code—people that my organization have identified. These persons are being kept on a string without their knowledge. All four are being watched from many directions to present your office and your team with weapons to help solve your homicides. Christian, we need you in forensics. I need Abron Kelsey in the field with me. Yours is a covert job. When one of us three brings you evidence, the results must stay between us and be handled quickly. Captain Saunders trusts you inexplicably." Jake handed Christian a small piece of paper. After opening it and noting the names of four people, Jake took back the paper and put a match to it.

Christian was stunned. "What's going on, Captain?" he asked. "This seems like something out of a fiction piece. How could any of these persons gain financially? And why would they go bad knowing what they would lose?"

"It's our job to find out," retorted Saunders, "with your help."

Jake then reiterated, "The information divulged in this meeting stays out of reach from any ears other than ours."

*****

"I think my exit with the professors went well," Isabel told Abron. "Something has bothered me through the talks with the professors."

"What do you mean?" asked Abron.

"They have pretended not to have met except at formal meetings and conferences over the years."

"And?" asked Kelsey, pushing her to the point.

"I got the feeling that they were more than passing acquaintances."

Living together as husband and wife in Abron's condo, the same gated community that Officer Pat Price was in, Isabel updated her husband. "Maria called this morning, wanting to meet for lunch. I told her finals were early next week, but I would take a rain check. She seemed overly disappointed. Did I do the right thing?"

"Izzy, this is the best path to keep you out of harm's way. Our gated community won't keep anyone out except those that don't want in."

Izzy interrupted. "I never thought marrying a cop would change the way I think. I now suspect and analyze everything that comes my way. How would Maria not know Elliot Carlson?"

Abron took a pause. He knew Maria was privy to the Rose Lake investigation. "Explain," said Kelsey.

"I slipped and told her you thought Elliot was playing a bigger part than he let on. She pretended to have never heard his name. That to me seems impossible, right?"

Again, a short pause from Abron. "Give me a day to run with that. In the meantime, don't get together with her unless it's in a public place. Izzy, I want you as far away from this mess as possible," he told her for the second time. "Involved people are dying." Abron hesitated then threw her off course. With a slight smile, he said, "By the way"—changing the subject quickly—"a couple of your old friends, Scott and Julie. called to ask if they could sit with your parents and I at your graduation ceremony."

Her smile and her attitude change told a story before she said a word. "I would do anything for them." She began telling Abron about her very long and tough journey. "Those two helped me through the hardest period of my young life. Abron, when I met Scott, I was literally lost in the deepest, darkest part of my mind that I could create. Losing everything at that age—racing future, the tour. When you're thirteen years old and your mind-set is clear, the accident was larger than life.

"From the moment Scott entered my hospital room that first time, I was in love. He was so full of joy and very handsome. So positive. I was truly smitten with puppy love. After that first meeting, I'm pretty sure he recognized the infatuation because the next day he introduced me to the luckiest person in the world—his wife, Julie. They worked with me for eight months of my life on a daily basis, bringing me back to a good place. Scott, my physical rehab. Julie, my mental rehab. I don't know what would have happened to me without their intervention."

Kelsey was awestruck at the emotional, heartfelt outburst from his Isabel. Matter-of-factly but with a sly smile, he asked, "Is that a yes on the ceremony?" She slammed into him. A few short words from Abron and she was turned on. Big time. Clothes went flying. Isabel had him on the couch before he could speak. His Izzy had turned into a sex machine. He had discovered, to his delight, that when she was emotional, a sly look and questioning answer could push her button.

*****

"Christian we need to meet with Shawn and Jake, ASAP, at the Davenport. I'm with Izzy, and I don't want her to get wind of what I'm thinking. Can you arrange it for tomorrow?"

The next morning found the four meeting in a closed bar with coffee and notepads. Captain Saunders, Jake Monroe, and Christian Caine sat listening to Officer Kelsey. "Elliot Carlson is involved with Rose Lake and our inside nest of corruption. Elliot has been feeding us with false information, trying to lead us away from the truth about the Nelsons. Basically, they were loners but not killers. Jake's mate, over at the Bureau, called me late last night about Elliot's past job experience. We know he worked for the mines in Kellogg and Wallace. Elliot has extensive experience with explosives. As a gyppo miner, he did his own dynamiting underground."

Without hesitation, Captain Saunders said, "A search warrant will be ready before noon today. Abron, you, Terry, and Christian show up unannounced."

"Would it help my cover-up if I was with the team, investigating Elliot?"

"Monroe's in," said Shawn.

Abron, with caffeine in his veins, was not through talking yet. "Ron Rowe discovered, while talking to the Snider twins, that the Nelsons were working on a way to save the twins' parents from losing their farm. That's why they purchased the land before they were murdered. Ron mentioned that the twins reminded him that the Nelsons were murdered before their parents disappeared." Abron went on, over the next twenty minutes, about Izzy's clues further implicating Elliot. He added his take on Pat and Maria's affair then started in on Cynthia's actions toward Terry Hollander when the two detectives ambushed her at the courthouse. "Let's not forget Tony Bara from CDA. Jake, your team does a thorough job. I was hoping that one or two of our own were not in on this," said Abron.

Jake Monroe finished the meeting by concluding, "Those four names need to stay under wraps. People are still dying. And now we have a fifth name to add to the list—Elliot Carlson. Possibly a collaborator."

Tony Bara and Pat Price were out at the Nelsons' farm by themselves. Tony asked, "Does Maria's assessment of Isabel and Abron hold water?"

Pat answered, "Maria's closer to Cynthia. Between the two of them, they see more of the picture. I don't know Maria except in passing. My talks with Abron lead me to believe he's suspicious of names within both departments. He's becoming more aloof to questions."

Tony commented, "We're so far past the point of no return, I guess two more bodies won't matter." The two deputies had met at the Nelsons' to check something down in the hole. When satisfied, they departed in different directions.

After Pat was out of sight, Tony called from his second phone. "Cynthia?"

"Tony, what's up?"

"Pat lied to me just now. He and Maria are hiding an affair."

"I wonder what else," she replied. Later that evening the assistant DA used her second phone.

"The troops are getting nervous. We need to meet."

"How nervous" was the answer.

"Deadly" was the reply.

"Chewelah, Tuesday evening." Both phones clicked off. They couldn't meet where there were cameras. That eliminated the usual hotel lobby at the Indian Casino. Both knew of the late-night café. It provided privacy through the placement of tables and booths in three different rooms. At eight in the evening, near mid-week, the café would be almost void of ears in one or two of the dining areas. Both participants were exceptionally experienced at projecting normalcy to prying eyes. Through makeup, changed hairstyles, and glasses, they were partially disguised.

"We need to start wrapping up this mess," said Cynthia.

John didn't like orders from anyone. "Dillon has been called in," said John.

Cynthia showed signs of nervous concern. "Have you sold any lately?"

John grew slightly more agitated. *How dare she,* he thought. In a heartbeat, John weathered his own storm, knowing that Cynthia was still of value inside the DA's office being privy to law enforcement movements. "Within the month, your final payment will be available offshore. Do not talk to Webb or Saunders about the Rose Lake case."

Now she, too, was smoldering. *How dare he threaten me. How dare he order me. I'm the brains without which this whole operation would crumble.* "Pat and Maria?" she spouted.

"Dillon and Dewey," he replied.

Then she asked about the hospital shooter's brother, Moses. "Are we far enough away from him?"

He answered, "Dillon," again. John then let some steam out of the pressure cooker they were in. "Hong Kong has come through with the purchase of twelve."

Cynthia pinned his eyes with her stare. "I want more money. Two-and-a-half million won't be enough to leave the country and live on anonymously for the rest of my life."

John knew it was coming and said, "Five."

Her last word to him was "Agreed."

It was a long drive back to Spokane that night for both of them. Cynthia was terrified of the name Dillon. John was outraged at Berdot. Both were thinking, *Too many partners.*

John called his silent partner and explained recent occurrences and the meeting with Cynthia.

"My involvement in this is strictly monetary. You sold me on the idea. I bankrolled it. Nothing more needs to be said."

'What about San Bernardino?" asked John. "That was my way of showing you I'm trustworthy. I would have never gotten myself involved if you weren't my brother-in-law."

"John, dead witnesses can't speak. I'll take care of it. See you soon," Laskowski said as he clicked off.

*****

Dillon had received $400,000 for his business down in San Bernardino. He was cunning and wise beyond his age of thirty-two. Dillon had made no large purchases and revealed no signs of spending any monies beyond his income derived from employment working in the woods. He had completed a twelve-year apprenticeship and literally climbed into a position of better-than-average pay while affording him odd days and hours of work. He operated a Caterpillar skidder, working in different parts of Montana, Idaho, and Washington as the jobs dictated.

Dillon was raised in the woods. Hunting with his father and uncles, he had acquired an expert's knowledge of firearms, camouflage, and a predator's deception. "That's a tall order," he said into the phone. "How long do I have?" He then said, "Impossible."

John quoted him a price. "Half now, the rest upon completion?"

Dillon gave the okay. "You do know, with this little time, they won't look like accidents!"

John gave the order, "Get it done," and clicked off.

*****

The next afternoon at Rose Lake, Christian and Abron were making a foray into the Nelsons' barn without notifying CDA. Both had questions about the underground rooms.

Abron was carrying. As the two drew closer to the south entrance of the barn, Abron pulled his weapon. "Whoa, partner" came from Christian. "There could be innocents, maybe even kids in here."

"This time I'm ready. No more surprises." As they both entered from the south door, the calm and quietness put them at ease. "Before we go any further. Do you remember when Elliot mentioned that two persons had attacked me? How did he know?"

"The same way Isabel and the rest of the world was notified—newspaper," said Christian.

"I really need to get a handle on this. The duhs are taking over."

Electricity was on, and the chain fall worked as intended. Once in the underground office, lights were located, illuminating the room. Tables with dead-end wires bunched all over them were the first thing to be seen. The report Christian had obtained from Idaho sheriff's described the lab equipment.

Speaking, Christian began, "This had to be the perfect drug lab. If the Nelsons hadn't been slain, this room would be virtually impossible to detect. The only possible lead would have been Elliot's statement about the odor that occasionally moved through his property."

Abron was wondering about the materials used to make the Methamphetamines, and if Elliot had lied again. "Inventory lists from here didn't indicate any large caches of chemicals or other raw materials needed to cook the product. Yet they have a dozen pallets stacked in front of what looks like a vent. I think Terry and Ron were right. The business was just getting underway when I walked in on them. The report also didn't mention the opiate-laced powder I tasted upstairs. Nor any mention of a trace down here."

Looking around the room, Christian was stumped. "Tony Bara left out a lot. He and his team paint a picture of an abandoned drug lab that hadn't been operating for several years. I'm not a detective, but I do know forensic evidence. There should have been traces of chemical dust on most of the horizontal surfaces. No mention of particulates in the air or tabletops down here?"

Abron then queried, "Did you find any mention of the air vents?"

Christian shook his head. "No."

Both men moved toward the stack of pallets. The four-by-four-feet wooden pallets were new. Just like the lab equipment, there were no signs of usage. "That's an awfully large vent for this size of room," said Christian.

"Especially since the intake port under the stairway is so small in comparison," countered Abron.

Jake and Deputy Sal Domenico had just arrived aboveground at the front door of the Nelsons' house. Abron had coordinated their search. Casing the outside first, Jake and Sal then entered with the sheriff's pass key. Inside the underground lab, Christian and Abron were removing the vent shields. To their surprise, the fan ensemble was showing hinges on one side with a latch attachment holding the other side in place. Abron opened the swinging fan four-by-four door. Lights automatically came on, illuminating a long tunnel in the direction of the house.

As Spokane Deputy Sal Domenico and Agent Jake Monroe were entering the front door, Abron Kelsey and Christian Caine were following the well-lit tunnel from the barn to the house. Both men were impressed with the size of the posts and perfect craftsmanship of the lagging covering the ceiling and sides of the tunnel. "It's like a corridor in a house, not an underground cave," said Caine. The officers came to a wooden stairway leading to a lightweight hinged door that opened upward and outward. Both were aware of the mini camera lenses showing their every move to an anonymous viewer. They entered the kitchen area above. A rookie deputy named Larry Glasscock stationed on the porch had just begun a second outside check of the house perimeter. As it was opened, Jake and Sal pulled their guns. The tense encounter was brief. Abron had hollered, "Sheriff! We're coming up."

Christian was the first to notice the extensive library in the TV room. "Most of the books are about the Northwest. Mostly history," he said.

Sal beckoned the others with a whistle and a hoot. "Check out this monster gun case." The deputies counted eight high-powered rifles, five large-caliber handguns, and three shotguns. Within the same gun storage unit were several boxes of ammunition for each weapon. Meanwhile, Kelsey discovered a small three-by-five door, well hidden, in the entryway closet built under the stairway. He and Jake went in.

A large rolltop desk stood in the small confines next to a small computer table. Jake didn't think twice. He automatically opened the rolltop with his pocket-knife. Both officers were dazzled. What looked to be two solid gold bricks were in plain sight along with several twenty-dollar gold pieces. Opening the largest sliding drawer, Abron found folders with banking records from three different local banks. "How could all of these valuables remain undetected since their deaths?" asked Kelsey.

Jake, again without hesitation, answered, "Bara and Elliot."

Outside, as the deputy was finishing his second walk around the house, he stepped on to the porch. A shot rang out, and the officer was thrown against the house. Christian was standing in the kitchen. Instinct made him glance out the window. Another shot rang out, and he fell to the floor. Christian took a head-shot and would never know what happened. As Jake and Abron rushed to the kitchen, Sal was crawling to Christian.

The concussion was almost unbearable to the officers as the barn exploded, throwing them all to the floor. The entire north side of the house was blown inward toward them.

No one within the remaining house was aware or able to hear the dirt bike racing away from the Nelsons'. Dillon was wearing fatigues with a rifle slung over his shoulder. His dirt bike had power to spare. Within minutes, he was able to disappear.

He pulled off I-90 at Kingston where he had left a pickup and trailer In less than four minutes, the dirt bike was hidden in the trailer and Dillon was on his way east. *How did John know they would be there?* he thought.

Dillon phoned Dewey and Penn Norman for a palaver. Dewey had found Penn working at the Lucky Friday. An ex-con, Dewey and Dillon liked his "less talk, all walk" style. Both had agreed that more help was needed to accomplish what was ahead. Norman was in.

*****

Within two hours, the FBI forensics team was hard at it. The area had come under their jurisdiction when the explosion occurred and Jake Monroe was involved. Searching through the rubble of the Nelson farmhouse and the hole in the ground where the barn used to be, two bodies were discovered inside two different freezers located in the basement of the Nelson home not connected to the tunnel. One looked, at first glance, to be of Mexican descent. The other, a male Caucasian, wasn't completely frozen.

After being released from the hospital, both deputies had called their wives to tell them about Christian and let each know that they themselves were okay. Saunders had already met with Christian's wife and kids. Officer Glascock hadn't survived the high-powered rifle shot to his back, leaving Shawn another unimaginable task. Crisis counsellors were dispatched to help.

"Two of our finest, dead. Pete Chavez dead. Elliot Carlson dead. Elliot was our explosives expert until now. Whoever's behind this is cleaning house." Terry, Ron, Jake, and Abron were talking.

Shawn interrupted them. "Have any of you heard from Pat Price? We can't raise him on the phone or through his car unit. I just got off the phone with Captain Croop, and she can't locate Officer Flores."

"They might have taken the money and run," said Jake. After the explosion, Terry and Ron had been filled in on the internal investigation he was conducting. All in the room were now privy to the infiltrators within their own department.

"It's time we arrested Tony Bara and Cynthia Berdot. I don't care where they are or what they're doing. Cuff them and bring them in," ordered Captain Saunders. "Jake, you take Abron and find Cynthia. Terry and Ron, find Tony Bara and Maria. Pat will probably be with them. You'll need a SWAT team. I've alerted them to your call. All three are armed and aware somebody is coming for them."

Tracking his phone, they found Tony getting into his personal ride near the condos that Abron and Pat lived in. When the two deputies got out of the car and started walking toward Tony, he hit the gas. The chase was on. Terry was driving; Ron was on the mobile to HQ. "Send officers to Pat Price's home. Tell them to be cautious. We are in pursuit of Lieutenant Tony Bara headed East on 90 toward CDA. We need assistance."

Captain Croop couldn't believe what she was hearing and phoned Saunders.

"He's involved with at least six homicides and possibly the death of your own Officer Maria Flores. She and Pat Price were having an affair. All three are involved with our triple double," said Saunders. Croop's team sent out the word to all units from Post Falls to Mullan, Idaho.

Across state lines in Montana, there was a phone conversation. "Have you heard the news?" asked Bryce.

"I'm listening."

Not allowing himself to say anything incriminating, Bryce started, "There's been an explosion at the Nelson farmhouse. They're talking about two officers being killed, four bodies all together. CDA sheriff put out an APB on one of their own, a lieutenant named Bara."

Bob replied simply, "That should give us some peace." The call clicked off.

There was a second phone call about the same time. "Cynthia, CDA and Spokane sheriff's are after Bara."

She answered, "I'll call you right back. Two deputies want to talk to me."

John was thinking that if Bara did his job, there wouldn't be any Pat or Maria to testify against him. *Cynthia,* he thought, *is the only person close enough to make this end in a bad way.* Bara could tell a fantastic tale, but only Cynthia, that bitch, could finger him. *I wonder if Dillon could get to her?* Then he thought, *For the right price.*

John was at his desk preparing notes for the two classes he had the following day. It didn't take much preparation because he had been teaching the same classes for over fifteen years, and history very seldom changed with time.

"What a way to go," said one of the new rookie detectives talking to Rowe. Deputy O'Neal wasn't talking about the fallen deputies, Christian Caine and Rookie Larry Glasscock. Jim and the other new detectives hadn't been given the information on Pat Price and Maria Flores being dirty cops. Internal affairs needed to finish their investigation. Officer O'Neal was talking about the pair of officers found dead at Pat's condominium—killed execution style.

Saunders needed to breathe more life into the McCoy murders. The recent Rose Lake explosion and deaths needed to be handled by the CDA sheriff's. The governor called again for a verbal update on both explosions. He also questioned where they were at in the McCoy case. Jake Monroe had gotten caught up in the Rose Lake affair. He was ordered to back away. The McCoys were broader in scope, being tied in with Chicago and union mobsters. The Bureau wanted him to stay put and help with the aluminum plant matter. Saunders conducted the meeting that morning, presenting plans and ideas on how to better bring the Newman Lake homicides to a close.

*****

Three days earlier; northeast of Spokane at the aluminum plant, shortly after the explosion

Fire was spewing from the open east-side wall and roof. Law enforcement could only watch and contain a growing crowd of onlookers while firefighters, EMTs, and ambulances were scrambling to save lives and property. Workers that made it out sat stunned and staring in amazement. The fire had spread to the loading docks and a warehouse just twenty feet from the factory. It was chaotic at first sight when the three investigators arrived.

"Fire department's in charge. Our guys are crowd control," stated Ron Rowe. "Watch everyone you can. Look for any actions that are unusual to you from the bystanders and uniformed employees." The detectives were on the loose in seconds. Four bodies lay covered near the ambulances. Terry quickly questioned the fire chief that seemed to be directing the fire fight. "What you see on the ground. Six to eight more unaccounted for, according to the workers that made it out. The fire is too hot to give you a timeline on going in. We do know that there are hundreds of gallons of accelerants in and around this loading dock and warehouse. Advise your men to continue to keep onlookers out."

Captain Saunders was on the phone with the governor. "I'm awaiting word from my deputy and the coroners for more information."

"Captain, your jurisdiction is looking like a war zone," commented Governor Orton, adding, "What about the FBI?"

Captain Saunders replied, "They are heavily involved already. The Bureau will tackle all bomb-related aspects. To answer your first question, yes, it was intentional. We need to wait for the FBI's assessment as to professional or amateur."

In 1942, the aluminum plant opened just east of Spokane, making use of the cheap power available from the recently completed Grand Coulee Dam. The aluminum smelting and manufacturing process needed vast amounts of electricity for the process. Bauxite and other elements used for the final product could be inexpensively shipped up the Columbia for a train ride to the plant.

In the early years, the bauxite originated in the Caribbean. World War II produced a greater demand for aluminum. The real spike for the product began in partial peacetime post-WW II. Aerospace technologies needed a strong lightweight metal called honeycomb stabilizing. Aluminum had found a home in all things air and space bound apart from the aluminum wrap found in almost every kitchen in America.

Shockingly to all within the Spokane Valley and Coeur d'Alene areas, law enforcement was instantly caught up in what they thought was the unthinkable: a premeditated bomb meant to kill and maim.

*****

Three persons were erased from the list Bryce had received from Balicki. The blast lessened his burden by more than half. Concerning the employee deaths from the blast, he commented, "I guess I got lucky," to Bob. His other assignments would be much more difficult. Bryce could foresee tough, one-on-one confrontations from here on. Meanwhile, Balicki was in touch again with Chicago. Pressure on him and Bryce was becoming formidable. If not an accident, someone was fanning union flames. Another meeting would be set for the coming week. His to-do list contained only one union member and a couple of outsiders. The outsiders would have to be dealt with through planned accidents. All accidents unrelated to each other. Timing and location would be used to insulate them from prying eyes and ears. He would need help. But he would accomplish the goal, no matter what. The union man on his list was higher profile. This he would take care of with no help. As always, he felt nobody needed to know.

His own people in Chicago were afraid to get close to Bob. Few had met him. Few wanted to know him.

*****

All five were seated together. The weather was clear but chilly. Abron sat with Isabel's parents on one side, Julie and Scott on the other. Ms. Isabel Kelsey was graduating with a degree from Eastern Washington State. Walking to the podium to receive her diploma, Izzy gave it her best, trying not to show any signs of a limp. Only the five seated together knew about her many ski injuries.

Late that evening, over dinner and drinks at the Davenport, she gave a very short and sincere speech to "her five," as she called them. "Scott and Julie, you know my fears and disappointments better than my parents. I truly believe the two of you together saved my life. As hard as that would be to top, you did by providing a glimpse into a future filled with love. The love you two share."

Jack shouted, "A toast to Scott and Julie!"

Isabel looked right at her parents. "You know you've made my life easy through your love and hard work. All those trips and sometimes journeys to allow me to race, year after year, throughout the West. Then all those trips to the hospital, bolstering my spirits." Jack and Grace smiled. Grace had tears. "Dad, you then did the ultimate"—there was a long silent pause—"although it took one of your famous investigations, you approved my beautiful cop, Abron, allowing me to discover a love like Julie and Scott have. Kelsey, you are the love of my life." All four cheered along with the bartender, the barmaid, and a dozen other persons present in the room.

Later that night, setting aside broken bones, bullet wounds, and concussions, Abron and Izzy showered together, sensuously washing and massaging the other's naked body. Hands were feeling everything. With hot water rinsing over them, Abron stood behind Izzy, then they turned face-to-face. Their passion turned to eroticism that lasted until sunlight made them squint.

*****

Bara was in lockup awaiting trial. Cynthia had been bailed out through an anonymous benefactor. The governor had sent his own internal investigation team from Seattle to Spokane. Next year was election year. He needed help and didn't care what source in his state it came from. The mayor, DA, aluminum factory, union, and sheriff's department were under a cloud of distrust. If that wasn't enough for Captain Saunders, he was now faced with the mysterious death of Gus Taylor, former CEO of the plant. It played out as a suicide. Forensics saw it differently. Gus Taylor had spent a lifetime around firearms—hunting, skeet, military. He knew the safety issues. To be killed accidentally cleaning a few pistols had forensics working overtime.

*****

Rookie Detective Larry Glasscock's life had ended far too early and abruptly. His funeral was held at a Catholic church near the center of Spokane and was attended by family, friends, neighbors, officers, and citizens. Larry had transferred from Portland, Oregon, less than a year before his death. He was not married. He was the brother of seven siblings: four boys and three sisters. His mom and dad were living. After the funeral, they would have him transported to Sheridan, Oregon, where the family owned several plots in the local cemetery. A somber overcast day turned a grieving day into an almost unbearable time for the immediate family.

Two days later, the Spokane area was again hit with the full force of mourning. Half the population of Italian Americans in Spokane and all of Christian's and Tammy's neighbors and friends were present. The twins, Cody and Jody, were held tight by their mom and grandparents. Tammy's uncle and aunt owned one of two Italian restaurants in the area. The other was owned and operated by Tammy's parents. Most of their customers were also present. Christian's funeral and procession afterward lasted several hours. Law enforcement and the firefighting community were seen at almost every intersection the motorcade passed through.

Abron, Isabel, and Captain Saunders rode in the second limousine behind the hearse. Saunders and Kelsey spoke to the crowd inside the church. A Catholic priest presided at the burial site.

*****

"No rest for the weary on this force," Captain Saunders opened. "From this day forward, we need to totally focus on the McCoy homicides. There is still no definitive sign that they were not connected to Rose Lake. I think we all agree that connection is growing farther apart. I'm dedicating two teams solely to find the perps involved. The head team will consist of Terry and Ron. Jake and Sal Domenico the other. Everyone has their assignments. Be safe."

As the room was emptying, Saunders asked Kelsey to see him in his office posthaste. "Are you married to forensics, or could I convince you to stay on as a prime investigator concerning Rose Lake? It would mean a promotion."

"Captain, you said McCoys over Nelsons?"

Shawn answered, "Jake and I are just making sure we have a clean house. Donnie Webb, through Jake and the Bureau, believes Cynthia and Tony want to talk. Both are facing life behind bars. Neither Donnie nor I expected Cynthia to be bailed before trial. Somebody posted the million dollars through a local bondsman.

Footage from that deal gave us a clear picture of a POI. The bondsman said the guy doing the transaction paid in cash, leaving a cell phone number and a mailing address out of Sandpoint.

"His face touts a beard. He wore large sunglasses with a baseball-style hat. Sound familiar? He's approximately 5'6", 150 pounds. We have a license plate number. Our trace proved it to be stolen off a car belonging to a couple out of Otis Orchards. Whatever we can gleam from Cynthia and Tony, will have to be piecemeal, one-on-one with attorneys present. Obviously, Cynthia is under house arrest. We have twenty-four-hour surveillance and armed guards surrounding her home."

Abron looked puzzled. "What will happen with forensics?"

"Kelly McCallum will replace you as a civilian employee. I'm speaking with a possible new department head from the Tacoma Sheriff's Office. She had put in for a transfer about a month ago. The Tacoma office gave her some incredible recommendations. Ms. Bradley has a son and daughter that will be attending Gonzaga next fall. What do you think? Do I stop negotiations with her, or do you partner with Jake and the FBI to end what almost finished you?"

"You just teamed Jake with Sal?" Abron replied.

To which the captain said, "Being careful. Sal has the knowledge to carry the team. If you want this to happen, I'll assign another rookie as his partner."

"I'm in. When and where do I start?"

"See Jake ASAP," Saunders replied.

*****

Cynthia Berdot was entering the courthouse escorted by several Spokane police officers. At the top of the steps, fifteen feet from the glass doors, a large-caliber rifle shot sent reporters, cameras, police, and bystanders into panic mode. Standing stoically, a lone Spokane police officer pointed at a window across the street, yelling "Up there, second story."

Cynthia had taken a hit to the side of her neck and went down. There were no more shots fired in the next minute. The police force was scrambling for positions, surrounding the building that the bullet was fired from. Cynthia was the only one injured. Her wound looked bad because of all the blood. She would live. Spokane police could not find the shooter. Too much time had passed before they could enter the building. Jake and Abron surmised, from the evidence, that the shooter could have taken a second shot. He had bolted instead. Theoretically, he knew exactly how much time he needed to make a clean getaway. Talking to the Police department and Captain Saunders, Jake and Abron emphasized how thorough the Perp was. "A pro, probably the same one that killed Christian. Ballistics should give us clue."

Later that same night of the assassination attempt on Berdot, Abron invited Jake to have dinner with him and Izzy at their favorite café/restaurant in Post Falls. Isabel was pleased to be with the two, even though she had been prewarned that Abron and Jake would be talking cases. Jake told Isabel about his family and the once-a-month visits he was allowed while working cases. Jake wanted to help further with the original triple-double murders. He and Abron knew there was a giant piece of the puzzle still outside of their grasp. Agent Monroe had received the nod from the Bureau to partner with Captain Saunders's office. He knew that Abron had already told Izzy of the partnership to wrap up the Rose Lake murders in cooperation with CDA Sheriff's.

Jake spoke to Izzy. "Your husband and I are close to putting a wrap on the Rose Lake murder investigation. When that case falls, the McCoys will follow quickly. I'm looking forward to that end. Vacation time is soon—six weeks to be exact—before reassignment. I'm hoping my family will remember me." Isabel offered up several questions before Jack and Grace came in to join Isabel at another table for a piece of pie. *Izzy is always one step ahead of me,* thought Abron.

The detectives got to work. Jake started, "We need to confront Bryce McCallen about his DNA at the crime scene. Past Bureau allegations, although none have stuck, include witness tampering, murder, even grand theft. His only jail time was for bribery. Bryce served two years in a federal penitentiary."

"This whole thing would have been easier if Bryce or Bob Balicki were dynamiters. But we can't have everything," said Abron. "Gus Taylor told our detectives he smelled two rats in Bob and Bryce. If there were any crimes committed at the plant, we were to look their way. You hadn't come to town yet."

"Obviously the factory explosion couldn't have been caused by Elliot," replied Jake. "The Bureau along with CDA Sheriff's searched his house last week and found banking records over the last ten years. Besides having several mysterious deposits annually for over $15,000, they located a wall safe that contained almost $300,000 cash. Elliot kept a ledger in the safe showing deposit dates and amounts that coincide with the statements. Carlson had notated two payments of over $100,000 that were not contained in the banking information. The real head-scratcher, Abron, are the coins!"

A surprised Kelsey said, "Let me guess, gold coins from the nineteenth century?"

"Yes, five of them worth at least two-and-a-half mil." Jake then asked, "Can we make it a long day tomorrow?"

"I'll clear it with the boss when I take her home."

✻✻✻✻✻

"His name is John Laskowski, a history professor at Gonzaga University," she answered. Assistant DA Cynthia Berdot had just cut a deal with her own workplace. It was signed off by DA Donnie Webb and the Spokane Sheriff's Department. Abron and Jake were already on their way to see Bryce McCallen when they got the call about twenty minutes out of CDA. They quickly reversed directions. The detectives were to meet Hollander and Rowe five miles from Laskowski's home.

When the two teams met up, Hollander spoke first. "Cynthia is telling all. Apparently, this professor is the mastermind to the demise of the Nelsons, Sniders, Chavez brothers, and our San Bernardino duo. He didn't directly pull the trigger on anyone. Officers Caine and Glasscock, Price and Flores, and even Elliot Carlson could also be under his deadly umbrella. He's wealthy, armed, dangerous, and also extremely smart. Cynthia warned of one professional hit man he uses extensively along with a second dynamiter from the Mullan area."

Rowe spoke, "Got the call. All roads in and out are blocked, two minutes for SWAT." The professor's home was in the center of five wooded acres overlooking Hayden Lake. After a fifteen-minute wait, the call came in from SWAT commanders. Lieutenant Terry Hollander gave the command. It was a coordinated assault with SWAT and the sheriff's deputies closing in from four different directions. Front and rear doors were battered in simultaneously. Smoke canisters were tossed into both entrances. Too late. All computers, file drawers, and munitions were gone. John had taken flight.

Through Jake, the FBI jumped into the fight to capture Professor Laskowski. Airports and trains were put on alert. Border security was notified to the north although on a much-larger scale. The outcome, after forty-eight hours, was the same that plagued the search for Abron's POIs. The hundreds of square miles surrounding Hayden Lake were crisscrossed with logging trails, offering thousands of miles in escape routes.

The day before, Dillon had gone straight to John's house after the wayward shot at Cynthia looking for payment and begging out of any further deals with the professor. Talking with John, he and the getaway driver were offered several hundred thousand dollars for safe transport out of the area. Dillon's mind held a map of dirt roads he had used for years. Transporting the professor would be slow but easy.

The following day, Jake and Abron were again driving north then east to Libby, Montana. Bryce heard the knock at the door, turned the TV volume down, and unassumingly opened the door. Jake flashed his FBI shield, and Abron identified himself with the sheriff's department. "Can we have a word?" asked Monroe.

"Explain yourselves," McCallen answered.

"You're under arrest for the murders of Phyllis and David McCoy." Jake wanted to say, "And other things," but bit his tongue instead. Jake cuffed him while Abron was reading him his rights. The officers made sure the house had only one live-in. There were no dogs, but it was home to a pair of cats. "What about my cats?" Bryce asked.

"Our forensics team will arrive momentarily with a search warrant and animal control."

McCallen knew his attorney would alert Bob. Balicki would have to make arrangements to take care of McCallen's list. On the way to the city jail, Bryce searched his memory for any hint of a connection between him and the McCoy murders to no avail. *Unless there were cameras in their house the last time I delivered a payment.* He thought about the splinter he picked up from the picket fence leading up the driveway. Not remembering seeing any blood on the fence, the thought hit him about washing his hands in the McCoy's kitchen sink. The skin he lightly pulled off to get at the splinter—would it still be intact after so many weeks before the murders? Again, he thought not.

Bryce had done time before working on a mob job. The reward for taking the fall and spending two years in jail gained him two types of reward: monetary and a step up in his organization. His alibi now was perfect. Flawless. "Six months from now, life will be great," he thought out loud.

The following morning, Abron and Isabel were enjoying breakfast at the corner café. Joan poured them more coffee and left the check. Then she paused and said, "There was a man seated over by the door that told me to give this envelope to Isabel when I delivered your check. But he's gone."

Abron immediately went outside to look for any sign of him. "He vanished," said Abron once he was back inside. "Can you describe him?"

"Seated, he looked under five-six, probably around sixty years old. He wore sunglasses and a Jaxon like the one Robert Redford wore in the *Great Gatsby*."

"Did you recognize him, Joan?"

"I don't think he's ever been in. At least while I was working. He was wearing a bright-blue windbreaker. Powder blue!"

Izzy was opening the sealed envelope with her table knife. "It's a warning, I think." Izzy replied.

Abron read it: "The McCoys were too close to the truth. Be warned, you're stepping on some very large toes." The note was signed: "An admirer of famous skiers."

Kelsey called Jake. They would meet later that day. Isabel was shaken. "I thought my part in all this was behind us?" Abron was shaken also. *Nobody is going to threaten Izzy, not now, not ever.* At that moment, the Newman Lake case became sacrosanct to Kelsey.

Later that morning, Abron drove Izzy to her morning appointment at Eastern Washington State College. She and Abron had decided that she would continue her education, studying for her master's in sociology. Abron could support them for a couple of years while Izzy was schooling.

Swamped at work, Abron and Jake were interviewing everyone and anyone that worked for the union out at the aluminum plant. Professional staff and deputies were searching the backgrounds of employees and related business partners for any connection to the McCoys. With Gus Taylor's death and the intentional bombing of the plant, Phyllis and David rose to the top of the agenda. Jake and Abron also had to build a case against Bryce McCallen and help with the search for a killer on the loose in the Tristate area: the hit man that killed Christian Caine with one shot from a high-powered rifle.

The bomb blast at Rose Lake could be traced to Elliot Carlson. This became evident when more explosives were found in a shed on his property. Jake and Abron had concluded that the aluminum plant blast was not at all certain. A second bomber was in the wind. The detectives noted that to Captain Saunders: "There is a second explosives expert. CSI has noted some basic differences between the two blasts. Mainly the types of explosives used."

Abron furthered, "Until Cynthia, our sniper shows up only on Rose Lake issues. Jake and I have found she had several connections to the Nelsons' case. We need to have a talk with her, now that she's opening up. The shooter's home base is somewhere along the I-90 corridor. Evidenced mainly because of the frequency he seems to appear."

"How many people have died in connection to the Rose Lake homicides?" asked Terry.

The statement left everyone in the room shaking their heads. "Christian and Glasscock have really opened a hole in our department," spoke Ron. Saunders gave them a body count. It wasn't pretty. The original triple-double was still active. Still growing.

✳✳✳✳✳

Hollander and Rowe, along with new detectives Jim O'Neal and Sal Domenico, were searching Laskowski's house a couple of days after the SWAT intrusion. All was quiet. Forensics had departed earlier that morning. Going through the basement, O'Neal noticed one finished room with a wooden floor. He called for the other officers. "A wood floor in a damp basement?" All four were on their knees, lightly tapping the wood and listening for any type of hollow sound. Sal walked to where a large desk was up against the wall. All four moved it outward, discovering a cleverly built, almost invisible, trap door. When opened, a light automatically came to life below the officers. Items found proved this was the 1890s train robbery merchandise. There were several hundred vials of laudanum, opium in powder form, and at least a hundred pounds of gold nuggets along with a compact electric-powered, heat-induced processing unit that would melt gold ore into a small bar form. They would later find a hidden computer disk listing the booty in the basement. Also on the disk was a list of names associated with the transference of the treasure from the Nelsons' barn to John Laskowski's residence. The names included Abron's attackers, Elliot Carlson, and the Chavez brothers.

Back on the main floor, deputies were discussing the find when a window shattered, taking Domenico down. They all knew the path of the bullet. Staying low, they pulled Sal out of harm's way. Sal was wearing his vest, but the impact of the round hit him hard. O'Neal called it in: "Deputies under fire. Professor John Laskowski's house. Need assistance and ambulance." Ron Rowe, slipping out the back door, was met with another round just missing him and slamming into the doorjamb. The deputies knew they were outgunned. There were at least two shooters lurking with high-powered rifles versus the detectives' handguns. Then a familiar sound quickly deflated the deputies' situation. They all heard motorcycles racing away from the house.

Instinctively, they headed for the cars and gave chase, automatically putting a car on each bike. This time around the officers got lucky. Jim and Sal spotted a motorcycle down within seconds from the house. The other bike had come down a small hill to rescue the downed partner. As the detectives drove closer, they unleashed a fusillade of handgun fire out their side windows. The motorcycle roared off, with the two perps, through the brush. Impossible to follow with their cars through the tightly knit forest, Jim and Sal returned to the downed motor. O'Neal said to Sal, "We got lucky. There's blood on the ground and the cycle. You okay?"

The adrenaline fading, he answered, "I'll live."

*****

Bail was denied for Bryce McCallen on grounds of the heinous crimes he was accused of. Robert "Bob" Balicki was now responsible for all things connected to the Spokane cover-up and bringing back the flow of illegal monies to Chicago. As he sat alone on the deck overlooking Flathead Lake, he spoke out loud to himself, "Just the way I like. Nobody left to fuck it up." He had already purchased his plane ticket and would be departing the following morning. This scenario turned him on. Bob was excited over the meeting, the planning, and the actions he would instigate. His mind wandered for a moment in thoughts of the Rose Lake killings. "I need to find this hit man that's rained so much havoc on law enforcement and keeps pushing our operation into the light." Balicki liked the mystery shooter's methods. Bold moves, no prisoners. *I could use a man like that,* he thought.

*****

A couple of miles up the hill, north of Avery, Idaho

An old abandoned log cabin was nestled among the trees next to Slate Creek. The area was located within the St. Joe National Forest. John was packing up and getting ready to be secreted away once again. An underground miner from the Mullan area was helping him. Dewey had four wheeled in, edibles and comforts on the second day. John could not have found better help. Dillon and Dewey were extremely loyal. Both knew the riches they reaped wouldn't come along again in their lifetime. Miles away, Dillon was putting the finishing touches on the plan. The next move would take Laskowski into Canada and later off the continent.

Dewey heard it first—a droning then a rumble coming toward them. In a canyon with only one road going north and south, the two grabbed all visible signs they had spent the night. As quietly as possible, they forded the creek into the woods. Hiding the ATV, they climbed up and into a small mine opening concealed from view by trees and brush. When the team of sheriff's deputies and FBI had cleared the area, orders were given to bring in the dogs. "They can't have gone far. Their truck, and supplies are in Avery. The fugitives are desperate and dangerous. Take it slow. One of them is an explosives expert."

John told Dewey, "I'm too old to spend the last ten or fifteen years of my life in prison. I would rather end it here."

Dewey responded, "I know these woods like the back of my hand. We'll be running when darkness hits. I know you can keep up. If you fall behind, I won't have time to help you, but I'll mark the trail out." Dewey added, "John, we still have explosives, a rifle, and a revolver. You can do this. We need to run. They'll find us tonight, trapped in this hole. We'll escape at dark. The clouds will shade the moon, and the rain will conceal most of the noise we make."

"My eyesight is poor in the darkness," the professor responded. John also knew his physical condition wouldn't allow him to successfully tackle the task of running in this steep terrain. "Dewey, I never thought it would come to this—my dying alone in the middle of nowhere. I have a conscious heavy with grief for all the death I've had a part in." After which he pulled his own hidden revolver and fired one shot. In less than a minute, the side of the mountain thundered just before the sun completely set.

*****

Abron and Jake were in a conference call with the FBI lab in Chicago. "Dynamite used in the factory explosion was reportedly stolen from the Lucky Friday Mine. The theft occurred two years ago this June. We were able to lift a print off one of the blasting caps. The print matched up to a miner named Dewey Oberg, employed at the Friday. Ballistics has determined that the same rifle that shot Christian Caine and almost killed Assistant DA Berdot registered uneven velocities and trajectories. The shooter reloads his own casings."

After ending the call, both the deputy and the agent were concerned with the potential danger hanging over them. The hit man could strike at any time anywhere. He had several advantages on his side. Most imposing, he or she hadn't been ID'd. They did know that one of the two or possibly both of the attackers had been wounded at Hayden Lake. At least one was losing a lot of blood when running from the scene. CDA's sheriff and Sheriff Link Mathias of Montana had alerted all hospitals and urgent care outlets within five hundred miles of the crime scene.

It was Captain Saunders who suggested surveillance of Dewey Oberg. Odds were, he would lead them to the more dangerous rogue shooter. "We know where he lives and works."

Two days after the explosion at Slate Creek and two hundred miles southwest of Libby, a charge was detonated nine-thousand feet down at the Lucky Friday Mine, Mullan, Idaho. The underground shift working at that level had been evacuated when the "fire in the hole" warning took place. Dewey and his coworkers had finished their shift for the day. The next team would muck up the results of the blast as they began their day.

Dewey thanked his lucky stars that the bullet had only grazed him. His wound had bled a lot but caused no serious threat to his life. He and Dillon were able to close it with needle and thread a couple of hours after their escape. Each of them had lost several hundred thousand dollars with the death of Professor Laskowski. The saving grace was knowledge of the how-to in recovering a large portion of Laskowski's remaining fortune. They would lay low, work at their jobs, and bide their time before going after the fortune. Both men had killed and would kill again to save themselves and the fortune. Up to this point, they were secure in the knowledge that nobody had identified them. Now there was DNA from the blood spilled during the getaway through the woods. Fortunately for them, offshore accounts didn't exist. Everything was cash on the barrelhead.

With the death of what the papers reported was "the mastermind" of the homicides and bombing, the pressure slightly subsided. Dillon was not relieved. His killing of a deputy and the assassination attempt on the Assistant DA would bring on the dogs.

Laying low, several weeks later, the partners agreed on a ruse. Another bomb incident could shift more man hours by law enforcement in the direction of the union. They decided that another foundry blast was too risky. The pair also concluded that If they were to retrieve the hidden cache, they would need at least one other accomplice. Dewey knew an ex-con that he had worked with in the mines. Penn Norman. Penn was a hard case and tight lipped. He and Dewey had already partnered in some illegal dynamiting. Reaping several large paydays. It was Penn that came up with the idea of insurance. Something of great value that could be used as a bargaining chip if needed.

Hiding out for several weeks put everyone on edge. They knew that quitting their jobs might send up a flag. Dewey's blood trail DNA wasn't a major concern. All three felt that unless he was cotton swabbed, no match would be found. They all agreed not meeting in public with one another was top priority. Going back to John Laskowski's house would be tricky but not unattainable. Using a message board at the convenience store in St. Regis, communications between the trio ran smoothly.

It was a Sunday at nightfall. Two rifles were positioned: Norman thirty yards from the front door, and Dillon on the road in. Under cover of a cloudy night, Dewey entered through an outside basement door. They had surveilled the house the week before for cameras or trip wires. He entered with little difficulty or noise. Turning the electricity off at the panel was not an option. That could trigger an alarm. A two-minute in-and-out was set in place. Office pictures and a few paintings seemed to be in their normal places. One was taken. In less than a minute, Dewey was running for the SUV while notifying the others.

Later, at Dillon's mobile home located next to the St. Regis River, they stopped. Dillon had inherited the mobile and land from his dad. It was used for hunting and fishing forays over his childhood. The stolen landscape picture had a hidden envelope between the picture and the backing. A key and the drawer's number were removed.

"John had a tendency toward Old Bushmills. Looks like the story he slobbered to me one night was true," said Dillon.

The meat locker was located next to the general store in St. Regis. The three found what they were looking for: fifty rare twenty-dollar gold pieces, six ten-pound gold ingots, and over $800,000 cash wrapped in butcher paper. The cash was evenly distributed. Knowing the ingots and gold pieces were dead give-aways, they left them in the locker. The decision was made to go back to work for another month before meeting again.

*****

Standing outside on the front porch, the petite young woman looked harmless. *Churchgoer*, he thought. Opening the door just enough to communicate, he asked, "Anything wrong?"

"Your car has a new dent. It was an accident." The woman's beauty won the day as Penn stepped out of his front door.

"Freeze" was the order. The small gal was holding a large .45-caliber revolver pointing at his torso.

A man stepped toward him from the right. "Don't disobey her," he warned. "She's trigger-happy, and you're too close for her to miss." The trailer park was in the middle of a wooded area. Balicki knew there were no eyes to worry about this time of day. "Join us. You're going for a ride."

"If you're the law, I've done nothing."

"Not the law," replied Balicki, "but maybe a friend."

They drove him to a safehouse, one Balicki and Bryce had rented a year earlier for private matters. Sitting in a chair unable to move, Penn began to show signs of nervousness. Balicki began, "I know you've done time and that you work with Dewey." Penn blinked and focused. "You're probably on their payroll. I want you on mine. Or you won't be on anybody's. Do you understand?" Penn nodded assent. "I need your help. My job is to clean up messes. I know there are three of you. The sharpshooter has the skills I'm interested in. Name and location now. Or she starts with your knee."

Penn knew they were dead serious. They had identified him and Dewey. The intruders knew about Dillon, only not by name. Since they located him, Dewey would be easy to find. Penn knew he was in over his head. Norman gave up the message board in Wallace and the last location of Dewey's and Dillon's whereabouts.

*****

Captain Mathias and his deputies were in place. Jake and Abron ready to assist.

Lights were on in the trailer, TV playing. Dewey was on edge after Penn had alerted him via their throwaways. Having been befriended by Balicki, Penn Norman was untied and allowed to use the bathroom. He quickly sent a warning text to Dewey then a second text: Trying to be friendly. Needs our shooter.

Three hours had passed since the emergency communications. Penn wasn't answering his phone. Link had decided it was time to raid the mobile home planted next to the St. Regis River. On his cue, the deputies entered from both doors. Dewey gave up without resistance. He felt secure in the knowledge that he hadn't shot anyone and couldn't be tied to the explosions.

"Link, the calls for you," a deputy yelled with an excitement to his tone.

"De Borgia! We'll be there in fifteen to twenty minutes."

Captain Mathias ordered his lieutenant to take Dewey in and tape off the area until his CSI unit was on site.

"Abron, Jake, this may be nothing more than smoke, but the call is about a house on fire in De Borgia, twenty minutes up the road. It could be our shooter."

Earlier when Dillon received the text from Dewey. He went into high alert. Working in his daylight basement reloading shell casings, Dillon saw and heard the SUV pull into his driveway right up to the front porch. Two strangers got out.

There was a man that Dillon thought looked like trouble. The woman was unsmiling and serious. Both were wearing long coats that could easily conceal weapons.

Jumping up the basement stairs, Dillon hollered loudly, "Door's open."

The woman entered first, shading the second visitor's hands.

Dillon was hard; Dillon was smart. He stepped out of the hallway to confront them. Dillon was also ruthless concerning his own health. There were no words spoken for that half instant before Dillon let loose with a semiautomatic sixteen gauge. The woman slammed back into Balicki. The look on Bob's face in that flash was one of confusion. Two more blasts rang out. Before the smoke cleared, Dillon was dragging both bodies inside and down the basement stairs.

There was no time to contact Dewey; but Dillon suspected Dewey or Penn, possibly both, for leading the two armed bodies to his hideout. He had a quick getaway plan that went into action. No time for gutting the house; a fire would have to do.

Arriving in De Borgia with sirens wailing, law enforcement could see the local bucket brigade at work. The house was smoldering, but not entirely destroyed. The fire started in the basement where the two charred bodies were found. Law enforcement would have to wait for DNA evidence to find the identities. An SUV was located behind some tree cover near the smoldering house. Within minutes, Link gave Abron and Jake a lead. "The car is registered to your local that oversees the aluminum plant." The thought was mirrored in both their eyes. *Maybe they are connected.*

"Dewey Oberg, now in custody, could be the link we need to find the shooter," noted Jake.

Abron answered, "I'm seeing a battle going on between the Rose Lake, San Bernardino killings, and union activities connected to the McCoys." Kelsey was holding fast to his theory. Agent Monroe knew Abron didn't just throw things out there.

"What are you thinking?" he asked Abron.

"How did the union rep find our shooter? Why would he kill them if they were on the same team?" Possibilities were exploding in his mind. "Jake, I don't think Professor Laskowski was in this alone as the mastermind. I should have told you this before, but I needed to see a few things play out first." He reminded Jake of the note to Izzy at Joan's café, giving a partial description of the sender. "It could be our mystery man in San Bernardino. That would tie him mainly to Rose Lake. He would have to be a longtime resident that lives around or near the I-90 interstate. He had a knowledge of my wife's skiing career that ended eight years ago. Maybe Laskowski and he were partners."

Jake countered, "This is what the FBI resources are intended for. I can get a research team to find Laskowski's friends, neighbors, relatives, and coworkers. A fast-track request."

*****

Before the fire

Dewey had sent a warning text to Dillon the moment he read Penn's emergency message, warning Dillon of the impending danger headed his way. Penn couldn't be reached by either partner. Dillon was certain Norman had been erased by the two visitors—the same two he had killed earlier. Penn was the only way they could find him. With one exception. Dewey was now Dillon's main concern. Taking no chances, it was kill or be killed from this point forward. Dewey had never been to prison or faced unrelenting questioning as a suspect. He would crack, and Dillon would be identified. "Dewey first. Then Penn's plan of insurance. He has two cousins that will help for the right price. They are reliable and unknown," Dillon reasoned. One of the cousins worked at the jail where Dewey would be incarcerated.

"I'd hunt down and kill Osama for that price," Penn's cousin commented. Two days later, Dewey Oberg was found hanging in his cell.

*****

Lieutenant Terry Hollander's wife, Greta, along with Isabel had become best friends with Tammy. The two wives did everything possible to help her in every way possible since the funeral. Their usual hangout was at one or the other of the family restaurants. Greta's German accent always spiced up the conversations. The trio became, unmistakably, the Italian restaurants' most valued customers. Abron, Jake, and Terry would often join them for an afterwork beer and dinner.

That evening, Jake had loosely commented that he hadn't heard from his wife in twenty-four hours and was sending an agent over to check on his family the next day. It wasn't an emergency as his wife normally took the kids to family or friends. They had agreed that thirty-six hours was the limit before agents were involved.

At the table after all were seated and dinner ordered, Abron was telling the three ladies that Christian's killer had been identified by an inmate that had hung himself the following day. The manhunt was in full swing. Both

Jake and he promised Tammy that the killer would be brought to justice.

At the Spokane Sheriff's Office the following late morning, Jake received the call from the agent sent to check on his wife.

"Jake, this is Bob Jones at the Bureau. I canvassed your house and am now standing at your front door. Your family isn't here." There was a pause on the phone, so Bob continued, "Did a walk through. No signs of struggle or foul play." Knowing the rules concerning Bureau families, he then asked, "Should I question the neighbors?"

"No," Monroe quickly replied. "Give me three minutes. I'll call you right back."

Jake didn't panic but felt it coming on. The emergency phone rang, but no answer. The situation became serious.

*****

It was late October, two weeks ahead of the first snow-fall in Whitefish, Montana. The new homeowner was enjoying a doobie on the scenic back patio of the over-sized house that looked out over Flathead Lake. The Rose Lake murders were a thing of the past. With one exception—the shooter named Dillon that killed Bob Balicki and his associate.

The aluminum plant controlled by the union was settling down into a day-to-day routine. Payments had to be made by the parent company to satisfy the EPA. Money finding its way back to Chicago was a trickle compared to earlier years before all the problems.

Known as an enforcer, David Rutherford was given help. Two heavies were assigned to him for the tasks that lay ahead. Working through the underworld of crime and mining for information in prison populations, David had a leg up on the FBI and local authorities.

Rutherford was under orders to find, question, and kill Dillon before the FBI could get to him. The news of Oberg's death signaled an enormous chance missed by Rutherford. Thanks to his connections inside, the union man found the guard that was responsible for Dewey's death. A second piece of information was made available to the union rep from Chicago. Jake Monroe was identified as a former problem for the Chicago underworld. David set his heavies to task. Leonard would try to get to Cynthia. Berdot was under house arrest, wearing an ankle bracelet and protected by the Spokane police department. Nothing Leonard and cohorts couldn't walk through. Leonard needed several questions answered, mainly concerning Cynthia's Rose Lake operation.

Mason would locate members of Dillon's immediate family and friends. Questioning a neighbor two houses down from Dillon's smoldering house in De Borgia, Mason got lucky. The neighbor was an avid fly fisherman who shared a love for the sport with Dillon. Acting as an insurance agent trying to find his client, Mason convinced the neighbor that an assessment of the fire damage to the house was the first step for Dillon to attain reconstruction settlement fees. Mason uncovered a name and a location of Dillon's only sister.

The entire law enforcement community was trying to find Dillon. David and his assistants had to locate him first. Agent Monroe was on a plane headed back to Florida, leaving Abron Kelsey to follow up on new information concerning Dillon's whereabouts.

*****

It was now almost forty hours since Jake or anyone had heard from his wife and kids. Captain Saunders ordered up some R & R for the area's close-knit deputies. Saunders had invited Terry Croop and Link Mathias to the Bump Inn. Both captains were told to bring along anyone who helped in the investigation of the Rose Lake murders.

Isabel had pulled some strings. The Bump was closed that night, even though there was a full house inside. Forensics had identified John Laskowski's remains. Penn Norman was found dead in his car from a bullet to his head. The round was fired point-blank from a .38-caliber handgun. Balicki and Debbie Landen, his assistant, had been identified as the two burned bodies found in Dillon's basement in De Borgia. Berdot, Bara, and McCallen were under wraps. The famous booty taken from a train robbery back in the 1800s had been given validity. For the most part, the who, what, where, when, and how's had been answered for Rose Lake— half of the triple-double investigations.

Jake, earlier in the day before leaving, had asked two questions of Captain Saunders and Abron Kelsey: "How was Balicki involved with Dillon?" and "Is anyone of us safe with a killer on the loose?"

Isabel and Abron had stepped out of the noise for a moment of solitude at the back entrance to the Bump. Izzy asked, "Are we normal now?"

Abron smiled and said, "Yes," before they kissed.

"Something's wrong. That kiss was half-assed. What is it?" queried Isabel.

"I need to find Christian's killer. Before it's over for me."

At that moment, the two were interrupted by a familiar voice. "Looks to me like Abron finally got to first base, maybe even a home run." It was the voice of Sergeant Mike Gwen. The celebration was taken to a whole new level.

*****

Rain was rolling across the wheat fields of the Palouse into Spokane accompanied by strong winds and black foreboding clouds. An explosion many years earlier in Coeur d'Alene was determined to be a one-of-a-kind occurrence. The media and law enforcement had completely ignored the possibility that it could happen again. Several members of a white supremist organization were arrested and found guilty in a court of law then incarcerated. Game over. Blasts at the aluminum plant and Rose Lake changed everything.

Captain Saunders had ramped up the security surrounding the foundry and warehousing, believing the Rose Lake explosion at a private residence wouldn't happen again. He communicated with Captain Croop. "Rose Lake is your investigation. Our department and deputies will help when you need us." The Bureau would also assist June Croop in related areas. Saunders' investigation into the McCoy killings and the Caine/ Glasscock assassinations were his teams.

Over the state line from Idaho, Isabel and Christian's widow, Tammy, were having dinner and enjoying a peaceful evening at Abron's and her condominium. Tammy's children were staying with their grandparents, allowing Mom some time off from the everyday shuffle. Tammy hadn't been able to sleep or be an everyday mom for months following the funeral. Abron was in Seattle, representing the Spokane Sheriff's Office and presenting a final report to the state attorney general concerning the Rose Lake killings and San Bernardino killings and updating the hunt for several people on the lam, mainly an assassin.

Izzy and Tammy decided to go to a late movie downtown. Heading home afterward, the two ladies were walking to Tammy's car parked in front of Abron's and Isabel's condo. A van slowed and asked for directions. When the two ladies came closer to the passenger window, the sliding side door opened, and two armed masked men were on the ladies in a heartbeat. The two didn't have time to react. Chloroform-soaked gauze was held to their faces while the driver came around and helped with Tammy, the stronger of the two women. Isabel faded within a few seconds.

As the van was driving away, one of the men punched in a phone number on his cell.

*****

The explosion was immense, taking out both sides of the condo and ripping through the outer walls of the adjoining homes. Captain Saunders made the call to Seattle. "Abron, I have some bad news."

At daybreak the next morning, Kelsey was watching investigators and fire department personnel comb through the carnage of what had once been their home. Captain Saunders, Terry Hollander, and Ron Rowe were standing next to him.

"We've located two bodies. It's up to CSI," said Ron.

A coincidence? Maybe. The stars aligned perfectly? Maybe. Dumb luck? A possibility. Or maybe all three triple-double murders came from the same source. The answer was still being evasive. Just when law enforcement in the Spokane Valley was beginning to breathe a little easier, someone somewhere was cinching their laces tighter and bounding forward with more trouble.

Deputy Kelsey was no stranger to interrogation. Through his own intimidating ways with a couple of prisoners, he tasked them with finding Dillon's family or whereabouts. Tony Bara was beaten until he whispered to his attackers a possible way to Dillon. Abron was on it immediately. Flying solo, he became a dangerous foe for whomever dared harm his Isabel.

Abron Kelsey wasted no time in finding Dillon's sister. The Lewiston/Clarkston area of Idaho and Washington is located south of the Snake/Clearwater Rivers basin. Clarkston in Washington; Lewiston across the Snake River in Idaho. The Snake itself begins in the Columbia Basin where it splits with the Columbia and Yakima Rivers, turning easterly near the tri-cities of Kennewick, Pasco, and Richland.

Dillon's half sister had lived in several different cities over her young life. At twenty-three years of age, she had earned a degree and teaching credentials from Chadron State College in Nebraska. Her brother had backed her financially over the course of her studies. Finally stationary, Ruth DeLuna taught grade school in Clarkston. Her husband, Jack, worked in Lewiston. Jack favored Dillon because of his easy manner and knowledge of the outdoors. Dillon called Ruth annually on her birthday and Christmas. His checks were received monthly without interruption from the beginning through her graduation at Chadron.

When Dillon showed up at her door, she recognized he was in some kind of trouble. He stayed to himself for the first two days, living in the basement bedroom. In that time, forensics reported on the DNA of the two bodies found in the burned-out condo. Learning that Izzy and Tammy weren't killed in the bombing, Kelsey disappeared within minutes of a morning briefing in Spokane.

Clarkston was about 140 miles south of Spokane. The emerging storm had turned from rain to sleet and then snow while Abron raced through the Paiute Indian reservation and into Moscow. Abron was charging toward Dillon's sister's home at breakneck speed. Izzy and Tammy could possibly still be alive.

*****

The brothers had both put in time underground. The Silver Valley of North Idaho contained several of the world's largest silver mines. Their dad and an uncle had been killed in the Sunshine Mine disaster years earlier in May of 1972. The tragedy untethered the brothers' ties to societies rules of caring and kindness. Coupled with Dillon's loss of his dad, the three cousins bonded. They against the world. From barroom fights to theft and intimidation, over the years they somehow eluded jail time. Two days earlier, acting on Dillon's orders, dynamite sticks were placed in six different areas of the McCoys' home on Newman Lake.

That morning, the Spokane/Coeur d'Alene Valley was involved in another high-profile explosion. The sheriff's department, captained by Shawn Saunders, entered a tailspin of confusion and negative local and national publicity.

The FBI's man in the middle of the sheriff's department had just arrived back the day before. In the prior forty-eight hours, Jake had learned his family had been secreted away and held in hiding until they could coordinate with Jake. A message intercepted through a wiretap alerted the Bureau to the possible discovery of his identification and family location. The explosion postponed his being able to stay with his wife and children. The FBI would handle their relocation while Agent Monroe hurried back to Spokane. Saunders had updated Jake and several of his deputies to Abron's disappearance. He included the vicious beating of Tony Bara.

The deputies had a ringside seat when questioning the former deputy strapped to the hospital bed. Abron was twelve hours ahead of them in the race to Clarkston. The intense winter storm negated air transportation. Alerting sheriff and police in the Lewiston/Clarkston area was the quickest and only way immediate help could be pressed to action. Jake knew a twelve-hour start by the resilient Abron Kelsey might be too late to stop the inevitable.

*****

Kelsey wasted no time in adorning himself with dark camouflage, using the time to calm his rage and heartbeat and making sure mind and body were on the same page. Revenge was put on hold until he had his victim.

The porch light flashed on, illuminating a young woman departing the house for the lone car in the driveway. Snow buildup was becoming an issue as she had to take a minute to clear the outside of the windshield. When the car pulled out of the driveway, the deputy moved toward the darkened house. Only the front outdoor light and a dim light from a basement window was visible from his advancing position. Winter conditions blocked out sound and sight. Abron used bushes and trees to hide his darkened outline. He knew the camo would help once inside.

Kelsey had his Glock and an eight-inch blade to use if it came to that. A dead Dillon would be a disaster in his search for Izzy and Tammy. The Glock would be his second choice. Not certain the sharpshooter was inside, Abron noticed a quick shadow of movement breaching the downstairs window. Driveway empty, neighbors tucked into their houses in safety against the winter storm, he stepped onto the back porch. Dawning his night-vision goggles, he plied the door. Unlocked, he secreted his way inside.

What happened next annihilated his stealth and confidence in assuming he had a surprise edge. Piercing strobe lights stunned him. High-pitched siren sounds made him freeze for a second. In that brief time, three shots were fired from the dark, all finding their mark and impacting his body armor. He knew that the shots were from a .22-caliber weapon using hollow-point heads. Fortunately for him, they were not Magnums. His body barely moved when hit.

Knowing the direction of the onslaught, he lunged forward, presenting a smaller target. Through the paralyzing noise and strobes, he caught a bullet to his thigh and a glancing shot to his left elbow. Slamming into his foe, Abron was surprised at his large size and quickness. Kelsey slashed his rib cage with the blade in his right hand.

Dillon yelped in pain. The bleeding man had never encountered a frontal attack so vicious. Kelsey brought the knife back across Dillon's groin area, immediately spewing blood and causing another painful outcry.

The shooter's only move was to bring his hands and small weapon slamming down on Abron's upper back. Weapon empty, he fell on top of Kelsey. The next move was so swift and calculated, Dillon realized too late that his attacker had practiced it many times. Kelsey stabbed over his left shoulder, hitting Dillon's left clavicle that painfully pushed the blade away from his chest. Within that moment of pain, Dillon's forearm was broken as Kelsey, now on top, put the blade to his throat. It was like being hit by lightning through one calculated move.

"You took my wife and Tammy. You killed my best friend Christian. Tell me where they are, or I will skin you alive as you lay."

Dillon answered, "I don't have anybody." Abron Kelsey slashed through most of Dillon's ear. The pain was meant to be intense and mind controlling. He knew that cutting different areas would start the initial pain over and over again. "Stop," yelled Dillon, his chest heaving, gulping for air. "I swear I don't know what you're talking about. Yes, I shot someone through a window at a farm near Rose Lake, but I would never harm a woman and haven't kidnapped anybody."

Abron cut a groove across Dillon's eyebrow into his cheek, narrowly missing his eye. Dillon begged for mercy. He knew the deputy was going to kill him. In that moment, he just wanted the torture to stop. "Laskowski had an accomplice that could be behind what you're looking for," he blurted out.

Abron stopped. "More or I cut off your nuts," he yelled at Dillon.

"Laskowski told me he had a brother-in-law that was his partner. I was never given the name. He said the in-law lived in Montana."

"Freeze" came a loud shout over the alarm siren. "Police, put the knife down and turn around now" was the next command.

"Abron Kelsey, Spokane sheriff's," Abron yelled as he turned to see the local police force, guns drawn.

Cut up, bleeding, and in unthinkable pain, a sigh of relief fell over Dillon.

Late that night, Abron talked to Jake Monroe, explaining everything. When they signed off, Jake called the Bureau. "It can't wait. I need that information in less than two hours. Lives are at stake. Do everything you can." Jake hung up the phone and waited. Agent Monroe had worked with the agent on the other end of the call for years. Jake's friend had never heard so much immediacy in a voice.

The agent back in Washington, DC, called in several team members at ten o'clock in the evening EST. All gave it their best for an hour and fifty-five minutes garnering the requested information and more.

Captain Saunders was given more information by the Clarkston Police. It was mainly that Dillon, from his hospital bed, confessed to the bombing earlier in the week of the house on Newman Lake. "It was just to throw everyone off guard, framing the union. That was

Professor Laskowski's last planned effort. I was paid well."

Agent Jake Monroe and Deputy Abron Kelsey were cautioned over the phone against a vigilante approach to catching Laskowski's brother in-law. Saunders was throwing caution to the wind unleashing the pair to find the missing link involved with most of the killings and bombings. He needed answers, and time was quickly passing to find Izzy and Tammy. Knowing he was stepping onto domain covered by Montana law enforcement, Shawn was careful not to let too many ears in on the probe.

The pair had equipped themselves for winter trekking and surveillance. They pulled out of Lewistown, Montana, on a dirt road headed up and into the Alaska Bench. The Alaska Bench is known for rugged terrain. Held in almost sacred regard by Montana hunters, it is a place where elk, bear, bighorn sheep, deer, coyotes, and large blue and brown grouse abound. Updated by Saunders on the wealth that Professor Woods might have, the pair saw the possibility of armed bodyguards and high-tech protection surrounding their POI.

*****

Alaska Bench, Montana

On the helicopter ride to Lewistown, Agent Jake Monroe was overloading a distraught, vengeful, and wounded Abron Kelsey. Kelsey knew the onslaught of information was necessary. Jake, in return, knew his friend had an overriding distress signal, banging away in his head: save Izzy and Tammy.

Jake had witnessed the results of Abron's raw, unforgiving interrogations—both at the prison where Tony Bara was being held and now in Clarkston where the shooter, Dillon, lay in custody with needles in his arms and at least a hundred staples closing his wounds.

Deputy Kelsey's injuries were far less grave. An x-ray discovered four solo pieces of lead in his thigh; the hollow point had split on impact. Doctors operated and took out three pieces of lead. The fourth would have to wait because of its small size and closeness to bone and vein. Abron left the post-op room twenty minutes after they sewed up his arm.

Monroe's contacts had located Professor Wood through his tie-in to the deceased John Laskowski. The two were flying into a homestead owned by a former FBI agent now retired. Once on the ground, Rob Sellers met them and rushed them into his ranch-style house. Jake immediately dispatched the helicopter back southward, flying low, away from the Bench. The three agreed that with the wealth Woods could have in his possession, favors might easily be granted by locals.

Monroe produced several aerial photos taken earlier before this latest storm front had hit using infrared vision technology. Several large dogs and at least three presumed bodyguards were identified. Surveillance cameras were assumed to be in place. Sellers and Monroe received word that help was on the way from the FBI. With more weather closing in, that help would have to travel from Missoula on four wheels. It would take several hours before their arrival. Time, as an enemy, was looming larger every minute. Two precious lives were at stake. If they were still alive. A plan was formulated that included just the three of them.

Rob Sellers owned an m2010 ESR. Proficient at 5,200 feet, the former agent had spent time each week discharging rounds into an 8-inch target. His hobby would help in the overthrow of this fortresslike hideaway. With the recon photos, they all agreed on his position. He would be Jake's and Abron's hidden angel.

The weather was once again helping in their three-mile trek to danger. Constant snow made the going slow but soundless. All three agreed that it would be a second silent protector when the assault began. Abron Kelsey was fighting through physical pain. The mental pain was much worse. Monroe knew that his partner needed to stay in check and focus completely on the op. During the long trek in, Jake realized that Kelsey was in his element. The assault would be swift by the deputy.

Darkness was falling quickly with clouds, no moon, and some wind. Sellers was in position, locked and loaded. Night-vision equipment was performing beautifully.

The dogs were the first hurdle. As they approached from a gully behind the house, both had crossbows loaded with dart tranquilizers. There would be a yelp from each animal. If the guards were not near, they could still be undetected after the dogs were down.

A vested Jake would then create a ruse near the front door, hopefully bringing all three guards out into the open. Abron would use his stealth and hand-to-hand combat experience to breach a back-entry point. When the noise in front hit, area lights surrounding the house erupted instantaneously. Motion detectors sounded alarms set off by the guards running toward the intruder. Jake was almost undetectable from his position. He would have to move to help Abron.

The alarm system created a three-ring circus effect. Everybody on the compound knew what was taking place. Abron had broken in, tossing stun grenades and smoke bombs in all directions. No sign of life or movement. Knowing the layout of the massive one-story home, Kelsey would clear it and find the basement. The butt of a weapon was slightly showing from a corner near the kitchen. Without hesitation, Abron moved in, disabling a slow and surprised guard.

Shots rang out near the front door and then burst open from the impact of a guard slamming into it from the outside. Sellers first shot had hit its mark. Jake had wounded a second guard out front with a leg shot. The noise and light show was amped up when a Lincoln Navigator came crashing through the door of a free-standing six-car garage. Jake got off a couple of shots at the radiator and tires to no avail. Within seconds, the Ute and several passengers were gone.

Clearing the ground-level rooms took seconds. Abron went down into a dark basement. No sounds. Night vision on, he found an empty cage with cots and a porta-potty. The force battered him forward as the shot rang out. With protective vest stoppage, he crouched and turned to see a much older and smaller gray-haired man with a handgun poised to shoot again. Like Dillon, he was stopped in midaction with Abron's two-step hunched lunge. It was so swift Woods couldn't react. Knife unsheathed, it was beginning to slowly pierce the professor's neck toward the carotid artery.

"Where are they?" came the feral whisper of death from Abron.

"I didn't kill them" came an agonized voice from the professor. "But if you want them to stay alive, we play by my rules."

Abron grabbed what little hair Woods had and drew his face closer to the eight-inch blade. The threatening tip of the knife was now less than an inch from his left eye. "If you want your vision, we'll play by my rules," commanded Abron. "Call off your security now. If either young lady has been harmed in any way, I will cut your tongue out and stuff it down your throat."

Woods could barely stand; he was shaking so badly. Calling on his cell phone, he became more distraught. No answer. He tried again. No answer. Kelsey's cell vibrated.

"They're safe. Both ladies are safe," said Ron Sellers.

Seller's position was within two hundred yards of the house. Seeing the escape attempt, he had put a round into both left-side tires. The Lincoln had slid sideways before glancing off a tree. When the driver jumped out and started to run, he was hit by a third shot. He would live.

Rob found the ladies trussed up in the cargo area where the third seat had been folded down. Jake, hearing the shots and crash down the road, continued to clear the perimeter and then entered the house. Kelsey was coming out of the basement with Woods. Taking the professor out of the house, Abron stopped, nodding to Jake in the direction of the fireplace mantle. Jake saw the pictorial tribute to young skiers. In the middle was a larger photo of Isabel hoisting three medals. The day of the picture, she had won the downhill, giant slalom, and the freestyle competitions at Schweitzer Basin.

*****

Book 2

Prologue

Double Triple

Tammy Caine had lost her husband, Christian. A year and a half earlier, he was gunned down while helping in the investigation of a murder case. Formerly, lead forensics deputy for the Spokane sheriff's department, Christian was ambushed searching a farm in Idaho. On this night she was vibrant. Young, attractive, with twins Cody and Jody, seated by her parents, at the head table. Twelve months of trauma help had been taken seriously. Tammy's mom and dad owned a popular Italian restaurant in the downtown area of Spokane. Her uncle and aunt owned another, equally as popular near the airport. Seated around the room were family, friends, and a few of Christian's former law enforcement partners. Tammy's mom had invited most of the people in the room. She took every opportunity available to gather her herd. Tammy's mother also knew that something was cooking between her daughter and a deputy named Sal Domenico. Sal had been hit by a round fired from the same rifle that killed Christian. His body armor had saved his life. "And he's Italian," she would be heard repeating to many of the guests. Tammy's mom was trying to cover up her mourning daughter's display of affection toward Domenico. Everyone in the room was glad to see her back to the outgoing, filled with fun person she once was. Tammy Caine's closest friends, Abron Kelsey, and his wife, Isabel, along with Terry and Greta Hollander, were seated near her.

Isabel was in the last phase of her education. Having earned a degree in sociology, Izzy was finishing up her teaching credentials and masters, from nearby Eastern Washington State College. Abron had just passed the bar while working as a deputy for Captain Shawn Saunders Spokane Sheriff's office. The FBI was knocking on his door. They were after his many skills spotlighted in the work of the previous couple of years in homicide. Abron and Agent Jake Monroe, working together were instrumental in bringing down two leaders of a multiple murder case. Agent Monroe had recommended Abron to the bureau. Terry Hollander had been promoted to lieutenant. He and Greta had begun the long road of parenting, a year earlier. Also present near the head table was Deputy Ron Rowe and his new bride, Vale. Tammy was mustering the courage to stand and introduce Deputy Sal Domenico to her guests when the night was shattered. A pickup truck came crashing through the restaurant wall, exploding on impact. Sirens wailing, the first responders were firemen and EMTs. The restaurant partly ablaze partly smoldering. Within that cloud of smoke, little if no movement, could be focused on by responders.

Book 2
Double Triple

Chapter 1

Liberty Lake, Washington

Quiet and pristine, Liberty is surrounded by pine-covered mountains with the exception of a wide flat swath outlet into the Spokane Valley to the north. Without this overgrown meadow, Liberty would look like it was set in the cauldron of a volcano.

Fishing for trout, crappie, bass, perch, and catfish abounded. Spring, summer, and fall boating and canoeing added to the playlist for children and adults. In the 1920s, an electric train was railed into the Liberty Park area located on the northwest side of the lake. The rail line opened up the area to thousands of people living in the larger cities of Spokane and Coeur d'Alene. The big band era was in full swing nationwide. At Liberty Park, a pavilion dance hall was built on log legs protruding from below. The pier stretched out over the waters of the lake. In the 1940s Sig's Resort opened to the west of the dance hall. Along with Sandy Beach across the lake, they formed two of the more popular recreational areas.

Within a couple of decades, golf courses were added, and a small housing boom began. The southwest area of the lake was home to a picture-perfect fen. Cattails, tall reeds, lily pads, sunken logs, and protruding stumps were home to turtles, water snakes, and even an occasional muskrat or beaver. It was early fall at the lake. Two siblings were fishing out of a canoe drifting a few feet away from the cold-water swamp. On this day, the sister and brother, by chance, would unlock a tale of dark times.

About the Author

The author was born in the late 1940s within Kirkland, King County, Washington. The author grew up in Orange County, California, and was raised in the city of La Mirada, ca. Enlisted in the USMC 1966, honorable discharge 1968. The author attained a private pilot license in 1973. The author is married and has six children and fourteen grandchildren. The author is a former musician in the rock and bluegrass genres.

CPSIA information can be obtained
at www.ICGtesting.com
Printed in the USA
LVHW051145040720
659731LV00003B/188